CLIMBERGIRL

James Porzelius

paperback ISBN-13: 979-8-9869989-0-9

Cover Art by: Carolyn Johnson

To my family. Being your husband, father, brother, son, has been the joy and the meaning of my life. Thank you.

CONTENTS

...it is through climbing that I learned the most important lessons in life. Hold on, but not too tight; work with the rock, don't fight it; balance is everything; and always remember to breathe.

SUSAN FOX ROGERS

CHAPTER 1:
LAST LEGS

The last time my dad stood up was a Thursday -- in the garage.

He left the bike he was fixing, walked across the garage, and reached the climbing gear off a high shelf for me. He set the gear on the floor and walked back to the bike. That was it. Nothing dramatic. Just the last.

Then he swung his leg over the bike, said he'd be back in half an hour, and rode off into the sunset. No, really. It was late evening and he rode west. In fact, the cops said that the glare of the sunset may have been part of the reason he got run over. The main reason was that the guy who ran him down was stupid drunk.

As Dad rode away, I dug out the rest of the climbing equipment. Harnesses, shoes and helmets were all mixed together in our sports cabinet. I sorted the gear and piled a load beside each of our packs. We were deep into our annual end-of-summer CBC week (Camp, Bike, Climb). Three days of backpacking and two days of mountain biking behind us, we planned to finish the week rock climbing. It was a tradition we had kept since I was a little girl. CBC week had always been my favorite part of summer.

When Dad didn't return in half an hour, I was annoyed. I

wanted him to help load the packs. Since I had done all I could without him, I headed inside. Mom was just finishing supper and Walter was lying on the couch, complaining about football practice. Half an hour later, we sat down to eat, without Dad. It was just like him to take longer than he thought on his bike rides. It was not like him to miss a meal. Mom didn't seem concerned. Even when we finished the meal and she started to clear the table, she didn't look worried. However, when the phone finally rang, she sprang into action. She snatched it right up, but then held it for a moment before she said anything. It was like she knew that she needed to hang on to that last 10 seconds of our normal life. When she did speak, it wasn't her typical, "Taylor residence" greeting that always annoyed me. She simply said, "Yes."

That was followed by another "yes," another "yes," and, "We'll be right there."

Then she did her mom thing. She like knew everything that had to be taken care of and reeled it off to us in one long, run-on sentence.

"Kelly, put the food in the refrigerator, Walter, close the doors and windows, it could rain tonight, Kelly, feed the cat and get my cell phone it's on the counter in the charger. I'm going to change clothes and get the keys. Meet me at the car, Dad's in the hospital."

I looked at Mom to ask questions, but Walter walked between us on his way to close windows. He never did what he was asked without a struggle. He closed the sliding door and carried some plates to the sink. Now I was worried. On the way to the hospital we learned that Dad had been hit by a car and nothing else. Getting out of the car in the parking lot, I looked over at Walter. He looked right at me; looked right into my eyes and had no expression. I could get no idea what he was thinking. I looked to Mom to see how she was reacting, but she was gathering up her purse and phone from the car and didn't make eye contact with me. I walked beside them towards the hospital picturing all the horrible things a car could do to a body.

CHAPTER 2: THE HOSPITAL

My expectations about the emergency room couldn't have been more wrong. I imagined lots of action and commotion. Maybe some screaming and shoving. We walked into an eerily bright, eerily quiet waiting room next to the ER. Mom went to the reception window. Walter and I tried to look through the inner doorway to the main emergency room. There wasn't much to see. The room was almost empty. When the nurse at the window waived Mom through, we followed. We saw a cop standing over a patient, but we were being led in a different direction. I fought back images of a bloody, messy body; visions of my dad writhing in pain. I was so scared that I slowed down when we rounded the curtain by my dad's bed. Mom rushed to his side and grabbed his hand. Walter watched the cute nurse walk past the curtain. I stopped a couple of steps past the curtain and looked around. Tubes led from Dad's arms to IV bags, and wires connected him to beeping machines monitoring his heart and his breathing. I scanned the whole room and saw Dad's clothes piled into a corner before I finally looked over at him. In some ways, it was worse than I expected. No blood, no bandages, casts or traction. He just looked deflated. He looked pale and small and helpless. There was a hard plastic collar around his neck, and his head was taped to a long flat board that lay on top of the bed. At this point, I didn't even know what was wrong with him, but it looked like most of the life had been sucked right out. Mom turned to talk with the doctor.

Walter walked up to Dad. "We're here," he said. His voice was quiet, but strong.

I just stood there staring like a total idiot. It seemed like everyone else knew what to do. I stood in that one place while doctors and nurses moved around the room and explained things to Mom and Dad. Walter bagged up Dad's clothes and collected his wallet and watch. I stood and watched. Walter looked a little pissed. As far as I knew, anger was the only emotion he had.

Suddenly, a couple of nurses piled some of the monitors onto Dad's bed, unplugged some things from the wall and started to roll Dad and the bed out of the room. As the bed went by me, Dad grabbed my hand and looked into my eyes. His grip was strong. He seemed to grow a little bit before my eyes; not quite so pale and helpless looking.

"Hey Kell," he said, "I'll be okay. See you in a little bit."

It seemed like I had been invisible until then, but Dad's touch pulled me into the scene. The next moment, Mom came up to me and put her arm around me.

"They're going to get an MRI, and then they will move him up to a hospital room. We'll go to the waiting room." I followed Mom and Walter out to the waiting area. Walter got some money from Mom and ran to the cafeteria. He likes his food, and he's not good at waiting. I sat down by Mom and felt like I was watching a movie that didn't make any sense. I couldn't even pull it together enough to ask any questions. Luckily, my mom seems to always know what needs to be done.

"Did you hear anything that the doctors were saying?" she asked.

"Doctors?" I replied, showing just how out of it I was.

"Dad isn't moving his legs. They think he has a spinal cord injury. The MRI will help them find out what his injury is, and what can be done. We should know something more in a couple of hours.

All my "bloody mess" images were replaced by one of Dad in a wheelchair. Inconceivable. Intolerable. Instead, I just shut off my brain and numbed out. That whole first evening was kind of a blur. We spent a lot of time sitting in a waiting room before we moved to another waiting room for a long time. If somebody explained why we moved, I missed it. I worked on a puzzle – some little English garden. One whole side was lined with a pink, flowering bush. All the pieces looked the same, keeping me busy for a long time. I vaguely heard Mom call the whole family and arrange to give updates. It sounded like Grandma and Grandpa would be flying out to visit when we knew what was happening. I occasionally looked up when Walter walked in and back out. He must have been walking outside, sometimes a cool cloud of air seemed to follow him in. He never sat down for more than a minute.

When Mom wasn't on the phone, she was talking to doctors and nurses. I finally found a TV and channel-surfed for a while. Eventually, we all ended up in Dad's hospital room. He was pretty drugged so there wasn't much conversation there. Every once in a while he would open his eyes, look at Mom and say, "Sorry." Like he had done something wrong. These were the only times he appeared to be in pain. That first night, I had no idea how he got hurt.

About midnight, Dad was fast asleep and Mom took us home. She gave us a bunch of instructions about breakfast and told us to lock up the house when she left. She packed a small bag and went back to the hospital.

The first few days of Dad's hospitalization were long, lonely, and strange. I realized how closely my parents had always supervised me, because suddenly I was on my own for most of the day; day after day. Mom stayed at the hospital most of the time. Dad had surgery a few days after the injury to stabilize his spine, and Mom always wanted to be with him when he woke up. Those last two weeks of summer vacation turned into the strangest of my life. Walter was doing two-a-day football practices. He went to practice in the morning, came home to eat and drink, (like, a couple of gallons of water) then he slept until afternoon practice. He basically moved in with a football player friend until school started.

I had a totally different schedule. For the first two weeks that Dad was in the hospital, I just got passed from place to place. Really quickly, I learned that I could (and had to) take care of myself. I spent the first three nights with a family friend. I'm not sure how that got arranged. I guess Mom set it up because they lived close to the hospital. They have two boys younger than me, and I got really bored during the days. Sometimes I spent a couple hours with Mom at the hospital, but I couldn't really handle all that time in a little room with nothing to do. Hospitals suck anytime, but hanging out by my dad, who was either drugged out, or busy with nurses and doctors, was unbearable. I was either in the way or forgotten in some corner. I don't know if Dad even knew I was there.

On the second day, I finally found out about the accident. The police officer, who had been at the scene, came to the room to get some information from Mom. He was a little older than Dad, and thin. But intense, and he seemed powerful. I don't think it was just the uniform. He stood straight, tall and tight, like he was ready to take a punch. He was formal and polite. He asked Mom to step out into the hall, and I sort of stood in the doorway so I could listen and keep an eye on Dad. He was fast asleep.

Apparently, a drunk drove right off the side of the road and hit Dad from behind. The cop was trying to be nice to my mom by telling her about the wreck, but he kept getting more and more angry as he told the story. He was so mad at the drunk I'm surprised he hadn't added a few injuries to him when they brought him in. The cop said the drunk had called 911 on his cell phone while he was still sitting in the wrecked car. He kept rambling about losing control of the car and said he must have had a blow out or something and hit a tree. When the police got to him, he was still talking to the 911 dispatcher and complaining about the car and the curving road.

After the ambulance came, a cop walked a ways down the road to direct traffic and saw skid marks in the gravel where the drunk had gone off the previous curve and hit Dad. He followed the tire marks to the edge of the road and found my dad's bike and then dug around in the bushes until he found Dad. He made the ambulance drivers unload the drunk and take my dad to the hospital while he handcuffed the drunk and kept him until another ambulance could come. When the drunk found out about my dad, he spun a new tale about trying to avoid a biker in the middle of the road and hitting a tree. In a way, it helped that the cop was so mad. I didn't feel like I had to have any anger at the idiot because there was plenty coming from the cop. I just felt so bad for my dad. And for Mom. She was crushed by the whole deal. I stepped out into the hall beside Mom. She was shaking when she put her arm around me. I watched the cop walk down the hall and into another room about 5 doors down.

The third day I met the drunk. I was sitting on a windowsill in Dad's room, staring out at the beautiful sunny day. It was so different out there than in the hospital that it didn't even seem real. It was like a big painting or something. Mom was asleep in the only chair, and Dad was zonked out on medication. He was going to have surgery the next morning and they wanted to keep him still until after the surgery. When I couldn't sit still any longer, I wandered out of the room and down the hall. I slowed down by the room the cop had entered the day before. When I heard the laughter inside, I stopped just outside the door. The conversation I overheard made me feel sick, and angry, and apparently, a little insane.

"Dude, man, I must have just splattered that guy. I was so blasted. You know, if I hadn't have hit him, I would have gone off that embankment. I must have been falling asleep. I could have really gotten messed up. I guess I swerved after I smacked him and ran off the other side of the road. Glad he was there. Man, it would really suck to be paralyzed. So, I get out tomorrow. Party?"

I couldn't believe what I was hearing. I was so pissed. Before

I knew it, I burst into his room. I was livid. His buddy stopped in mid-sentence and the drunk looked up at me. He looked fine. I didn't see a scratch on him. Greasy hair was matted on his head, but his face was clear, and young and healthy looking. He repositioned his legs (which moved just fine!) and the little blue hospital traction socks stuck out from the bottom of the bed that was too short for his long, lanky body.

I thought of my dad stuck in a hospital bed with some inflatable cast-like things on his legs, unable to move anything but his arms. I just wanted to slam this jerk. I saw a cane sitting beside his bed and pictured myself grabbing it and breaking it over his head. I really wanted to do that. I imagined the feel of the cane in my hand, the sharp thunk as it cracked over his head, and the "umph" that would come out of his mouth on impact. And that was it. Once I started imagining things, I went into one of my spacey things. Instead of smashing the guy with his cane, I was remembering stupid, family stories. I stood right there in the middle of the room. I didn't say anything. I didn't reach for the cane. Because I'm Kelly Taylor, I did what I do. I spaced into a memory.

While my body stood in front of the drunk and his buddy, my imagination had me in the van with my family, pulling into a fast-food drive-thru after a mountain bike ride. A line of cars extended into the parking lot. Dad pulled in behind the last car and then got out to adjust one of the bikes on the rack. The cars in front of us pulled forward and, just as he was getting back into the van, a little car came whipping through the parking lot and pulled into the line in front of us. Dad lost it, which is unusual for him. I had heard him cuss a couple of times, and once he really got pissed and flipped over a big recliner chair in our family room. But he rarely showed any anger.

In my memory, Walter and I watched for Dad's reaction to being cut off. We leaned forward to watch as Dad jumped out of the van and walked up to the driver's window of the little car. Mom yelled, "Don't..." as he got out, but I'm sure he didn't hear her. He walked up to the little car and just stood there by the driver's window looking straight forward. He stood there for a long time, then turned, said something to the driver and walked back with this big, goofy smile on his face.

He got in the van and closed the door. Mom glanced nervously back at us, then back at Dad and asked, "Well?"

He kind of chuckled, "Well, I was so pissed but I didn't know what I was going to say." He glanced back at us. "When I got up there, I just wanted to kick the sideview mirror off of their car."

Mom looked back at us again.

"I knew I couldn't do that, but I really wanted to. I pictured that mirror bouncing across the drive. Then I realized I had to say something. I just looked at this terrified woman and said, 'that was very inconsiderate.'"

He looked back at us still smiling. "What a dork."

While he was talking the little car pulled out of the line and drove away. Dad chuckled.

"Well, it worked. But dang I feel stupid."

Suddenly I realized I was still standing in the drunk's hospital room. I wouldn't be surprised if drool was running down my lip. I had been there for a while now. Both of the guys were just watching me stare into space. Talk about a dork.

"Well?" the visitor finally said.

I was so mad. But what could I do? What he had done was way past inconsiderate. I looked at him again. Really looked at him. Stared straight into his eyes. They were cold at first, icy blue, but I burned through them. I could see them change as he tried to look back at me. He fidgeted a little, pulled a piece of straggly hair away from his eyes, then looked away. Scared. Scared of a little girl. Scared unless he was drunk. Screw him, I thought. Even paralyzed, my dad was so much better off than this jerk. I shook my head and turned and walked out. I actually smiled thinking of what my dad would say about my dorky move, but I never planned to tell him.

When I walked out of his room, I almost ran smack into Mom. She glanced into the room and then turned a quizzical look on me. I just smiled, probably that same stupid smile that Dad had at the drive-thru and scurried into Dad's room. My smile was sucked away into the sadness of his quiet, still room.

We were all at the hospital on the day of the surgery. We took over a section of the waiting room trying to kill five hours with nothing to do and without talking about Dad's surgery. Grandma and Grandpa were there and Aunt Joan. The surgery would take several hours and there was nothing we could do, but we all felt like we had to stay the whole time. Whenever anyone slipped away to get food or to go for a walk, they came back with this questioning look, as if we might have heard something while they were away. One of us would just shake a head and we'd all go back to doing nothing. After several hours, the surgeon finally came in. He told us what we needed to know. "The surgery went well." But nothing else. He was like a robot. No emotion, no expression. I really tried to see his eyes and his face so I could tell how things really went. But there was nothing. He could have been reading names out of the phone book. Just the facts, or anyway, what he wanted us to think the facts were. They cleaned out the space around the spinal cord, fused his spine with some "hardware" and screws and he would be heading to the recovery room soon.

Only Mom saw him that evening. He was sick and sleepy, coming out of the anesthesia. The next day, he was more awake. They measured him for a brace and said it would be ready the next day. Once he had the brace, they could sit him up. That news brought a little spark back to his eyes.

That night, Mom came home for the first night since Dad's wreck. That meant I got to go home for a night also. Mom looked so tired. She soaked in the bath for an hour, and I tried to help make supper to give her a little break. The next day, I packed a suitcase and moved in with my friend Sierra. Three days later, I got one night at home with Mom. Then I repacked and went to Leah's house for a couple nights. We repeated that pattern for about two weeks. Then Dad was moved to a rehabilitation unit.

Treatment really changed in rehab. Instead of lying in bed waiting for surgeries, Dad was up every day doing physical therapy. He got to wear clothes again and didn't seem nearly as sick, although, for the first few days, he puked every time they helped him sit up. By the time he got to rehab, all the medical stuff was pretty well settled and Dad was busy with therapy much of the day. Still, it wasn't a great place to hang out. It didn't have the same medicinal, hospital smell, but it often smelled from puke in Dad's room, or pee from some of the other patients. The worst part was the other patients. There was a guy with a broken neck who had a metal frame bolted into his head to hold his head straight. Most of the patients were old and had trouble talking and eating. Whenever they saw me with Dad, the shook their heads and whispered to each other. The nurses were the same way. Even though these people were all messed up, missing arms and legs and stuff, they looked at me like I was the real loser.

The one time I was there for a meal, some old lady puked all over the table where three other patients were trying to eat. There were a lot of patients who didn't look like they knew what was going on. I suppose I should have been thankful that Dad wasn't in worse shape, but mostly, I just wanted to be anywhere else, which worked out okay because school started the day after Dad went to rehab.

CHAPTER 3: THE ROCK

The first day of school was always kind of a big deal at our house. This year should have been the biggest. Walter was starting high school and I was going to my first year of middle school. But Dad was starting rehab and Mom was working extra hours. As soon as Dad got settled into rehab, the staff sent Mom home and told her to get some rest. Yeah right. My mom is the kind of person who figures out what has to be done and then she just does it. Her boss offered to give her some more time off. Instead, she asked them to increase her hours for a few weeks. She saw that we were going to have financial problems and she just dove in to attack the problem. For the first three weeks of Dad's rehab, Mom worked overtime. During the last week, she was back at the hospital getting trained to help Dad at home.

So, on my first day of middle school, Dad was in rehab and Mom was at work before I got up. Walter was trying to act cool, like starting high school was no big deal. I tried to keep things a little normal. Our first day of school tradition had been a special breakfast, followed by the annual videotaping. Mom would tape me and Walter walking around from behind the big chair in our living room. We would come to the front of the chair, talk about our new grade and teacher and friends, and then walk around to the back of the chair. Her plan was to edit the tapes together so that it would look like we were just walking around the chair and growing a year each time we went around the back. This year, I got up as soon as Mom left for work and I made a coffee cake. I got up as soon as Mom left for work and I made a coffee cake. I got the camera out and set it up in front of the chair. I thought it was a weak effort until I pulled the coffee cake out of the oven and that warm, fresh baking smell filled the kitchen. For a brief moment, I had a little hope. Walter, of course, slept until the last possible minute. I was sitting at the table finishing my breakfast when he came out to the kitchen.

"Nice," he said as he grabbed a piece of coffee cake. Crumbs dropped across the floor as he walked to the cupboard and pulled out a glass. He stood at the counter and washed his cake down with a glass of orange juice. With his mouth half full, he looked over at the camera set up and smiled.

"I don't think so," he said. A car honked and he grabbed his backpack and was out the door. No "goodbye," no "good luck with middle school," nothing. I sat at the table and listened to the slam of the door echo around the empty house. For the first time since Dad's injury, I cried. Just me at the table with a stupid coffee cake and a camera with no one to record. I sat and sobbed for an hour and twenty-three minutes. I know cuz I was late for school. From that moment on, I avoided the house as much as I possibly could.

With Walter in football and school, and Mom working extra, avoiding the empty house was a bit of a challenge. At first, I delayed coming home from school as much as possible. I went to a friend's house when I could, but I'd spent a lot of time at other people's houses when Dad was first hospitalized. I was tired of being with other kid's families but I didn't want to be home alone. I started riding my bike a lot after school. I explored every possible route from school to home. A couple of times I rode over to the hospital. I had an idea which window was Dad's, and I would stop outside the hospital and watch his window. Nothing ever happened there, so one day I rode out where Dad had been injured. There wasn't much to see there either, and I got really nervous whenever a car came around a curve. I pulled way off the road and sat there thinking about Dad's injuries and the things he couldn't do. I was so glad we had done the backpacking and mountain bike riding, and I thought about how close we had been to two days of rock climbing. Dad used to rock climb a lot. I was just starting to get into it. I sat there wondering if I would ever get to climb again. Then I remembered the Ravine.

The Ravine is a small canyon just outside of town where locals rock climb and boulder. Most of the climbs are really good, but really short, so they are perfect for bouldering. That's climbing close to the ground on really difficult moves and it's perfect for me because you don't need anyone with you to work a rope. For the first time since Dad's injury, I felt something positive. Some little tingle of excitement. I could go to the Ravine by myself. I couldn't get Dad out there yet, but I knew I would. Meanwhile, I could still climb.

The next day, I carried a small pack to school with a water bottle, a snack, and my climbing shoes. After school, I headed out to the Ravine on my bike. I rode up to the older section of town where the lawns and trees are big; really different than the tiny treeless lots where we live. The trail to the Ravine winds through an old apple orchard just as it leaves town.

The apple orchard is one of my favorite places, even though it kind of makes me feel sad. I like it because it's alive and a little wild since no one takes care of it anymore. Every time I ride through it, I think of the people who must have planted it long before I was born. I think of all the years that people tended the trees and picked luscious, ripe apples off the branches. I feel a little sad because no one takes care of the little orchard anymore. I wonder why no one cares about the trees or the apples anymore. On the other hand, I think I like the orchard better a little wild.

I rode into the orchard dodging fallen apples that littered the ground. The sweet, musty smell of rotting fruit hung thick over the trail. Flies and bees buzzed the downed fruit. At the far end of the orchard, I rolled my bike up and down a series of whoop-de-doos, then plummeted down through a ditch before ramping up into the woods on a steep section of trail.

My old mountain bike was perfect for that trail. It wasn't the best looking bike in town,

the frame had been spray painted black by some previous owner, and bright teal showed through the many scratches, but Dad had replaced almost all the moving parts. He was really into bikes and still has quite a collection. The whole bunch is probably not worth much to anyone but him. He specialized in buying used, beat up bikes and fixing them up so they ran well. He was always bringing home junk bikes from police auctions or thrift shops. After mixing and matching parts to get one bike working well, he sold it or gave it away. He got hit on one of those bikes; an old Raleigh 10-speed. Dad claimed it was just like the one he'd had in high school. It did look a bit like an antique with a leather seat and no bottle holder. That was the bike I watched him hop on and ride away...

I shook off the memory and focused on the trail. I was a little nervous about finding my way out to the Ravine. I had been there last year with Dad, but we drove in from another direction; on an old fire road in Dad's old four-wheel-drive truck. I had a general idea where it was and was pretty sure the trail would get me there. I figured I couldn't get too lost, because it was uphill away from town, and I could always just aim downhill to find my way back. Getting lost didn't worry me too much. The stories I'd heard about Strider worried me a lot. Strider is our local homeless guy and some people said he lived out here along this trail.

Actually, we have two homeless guys (it's a pretty small town). One is your average homeless guy who spends a lot of time drunk and must have a place to stay sometimes, but he's on the street a lot. The other guy is something else. My friends call him "Strider" like the guy in "Lord of the Rings". There is only a slight resemblance. He always wears a long black coat, fingerless gloves, and he has long hair. But, there is nothing handsome about our Strider. I think he is a white man but his face and hands are black because he lives outside and apparently never, ever washes. I've never seen him talk. He rides around town on an old black bike and picks up cans for recycling. The closest I had ever come to him was in a bike shop with my dad. The clerk suddenly left us, reached behind the counter, and picked up a large plastic bag full of empty cans. He came walking up to me like he was going to hand it to me. I was really confused for a second. Then, he started to lift it over my head to someone behind me. I turned and looked up and Strider stood right behind me. He was so freaky that I would have screamed, but I couldn't make any noise at all. He just reached over my head and grabbed the bag. I struggled to breath; partly because I was so scared, partly because he was veiled in this cloud of thick, pungent smell. Some mixture of smoke and sweat and, I think, old dead things. Luckily, most of the odor followed him back out the door. Nobody in the store said anything, they just all went back to business.

Some people say they've talked with him. That doesn't sound very believable to me. One kid at school said Strider was a big shot lawyer in California and just left everything to come up here and live on the street. Another said that Strider jumped up on the hood of his car when they were stopped at a light late one night. A lot of people say that he lives in these woods just past the old apple orchard. Right. But like the other stories, I didn't really believe it. I was, however, a little nervous about finding my way to the Ravine, and about running into Strider. I was remembering all the stories I had heard about him when I left the orchard and took the trail into the woods. I dipped through a gully and started up a long climb. A small, flat trail took off to one side and I looked at it for a while trying to decide if it was the right way. I finally started riding the flat trail, watching for any place to turn further uphill. After about a mile I saw a faint trail to the left. I got off my bike and left it by a tree that had fallen across this little trail. I thought I'd walk ahead a little ways to see if the trail went anywhere before I tried to lift my bike over the tree. I walked past a few branches that kind of obscured the trail and came to a little camp. Piles of blankets lay under the boughs of a tree where someone had been sleeping. A couple of pans sat next to a fire ring. Then, I saw the bike. This was his camp! His home. Strider never went to town without his bike. That meant he was here.

At that same moment I knew he was not only here -- but he was watching me. I could feel him watching me. That strange, dark, musty, dead smell started to drown out the fresh forest scent. I wanted to run but I didn't know which direction to go. Slowly I looked around. The camp was eerily quiet; no twittering birds, no rustling leaves. A silent breeze intensified the strange smell. Every shadow seemed to move. Every tree branch looked like a long black coat fluttering in the breeze. I really wanted to get out of there. I took one last look around then turned to head directly back to my bike. The trail ahead seemed black. I thought I'd turned the wrong way and was facing directly into a tree. Then it moved. It was him. Big, black and scary as a nightmare. I looked up into his chest. Then, on higher up into his eyes. He had no expression. He made no sound. I stood, stunned for what seemed like an eternity. I didn't know what to do. The smell completely saturated my lungs, even though I swear I wasn't breathing. He didn't seem to want anything but he was blocking the trail. Finally, I reached into my pocket and pulled out an energy bar. I didn't know why. I just held it out to him. He reached out a big, black, crusty hand and took my bar. Then he stood watching me. I stepped to the side of the trail, and he walked past me and into his camp. I scurried back to my bike, grabbed it and rode out of there faster than I had ever ridden before.

I don't think I took a breath until I was half a mile down the trail. Then I started shaking. I stopped beside a small stream and got off my bike. I splashed some water on my face and looked back up the trail. Holy Crap! I couldn't believe I had just walked into Strider's camp. I gave him an energy bar. What's up with that? I started laughing, or making some sort of cackling noise, while I shook and sucked for air, sitting there on a rock in the middle of the woods all by myself. I realized the energy bar thing came from my dad.

Once when we were in Portland, he saw a homeless woman by the edge of the road. While we sat at the light, he looked around the car for something to give her. I thought he was looking for his billfold but he picked up an energy bar, opened his window and handed it to her when she walked up. Then we all had to listen to him for the next half hour talking about what a great plan that was. Instead of a dollar, he would always give beggars an energy bar. He said they probably needed something to snack on while they were out in the street all day. He said that he would want an energy bar if he were out there. He noted that they were individually wrapped so they were safe to eat, and they probably couldn't be traded for booze. He decided to carry energy bars whenever we went to a city. From then on, he always handed them out whenever he saw a homeless person or a beggar. I guess it had just become a reaction for me too.

Eventually, I got back on my bike and found my way to the bouldering area. It wasn't far from the stream where I had stopped. Before I got to the actual rock, I could hear voices and clanging gear (I love that sound). I ditched my bike in a bush by a parking area and carried my little pack down a steep trail to the climbing area. A bunch of high school and college age guys were there. At first I was glad, cuz I was still freaked out about my encounter with Strider, and I felt safer with these guys around. Soon, however, I saw that they all seemed to know each other, and they looked like they knew what they were doing. Like they climbed there a lot. I wasn't a very good climber, and the last thing I wanted was a bunch of older guys watching me try to climb. I walked around by the edge of the climbing area and tried to check out some climbs without attracting any attention to myself. Sitting on a small boulder, I pulled my climbing shoes out of the pack and slipped them on. When the guys all seemed focused on a climb that someone was struggling on, I tried one move by the edge. Amazingly, I pulled it and kept climbing a little ways up and mostly to the left so I wouldn't get too high off the ground. I love climbing and got really focused on what I was doing. After making several moves, I got to a place that was kind of overhanging. I was about to drop when a voice directly behind me said, "Go for it, I got you". One of the guys had moved behind me and had his hands right behind my shoulders to catch me if I fell. I was a little freaked. I made a half-hearted attempt to pull the move and fell. The guy caught my shoulders and let my feet fall to the ground. He was way strong. It felt like he could have tossed me back up to the overhang with ease. He held my shoulders until I was solid on my feet. He smelled a little of sweat, but his was not an old, dead smell. He smelled of strength and life.

"Looky here. It's Katie Brown" said one of the guys.

"Nice job Katie" said the guy who caught me.

I think I mumbled "thanks" and slipped away. I knew from my dad that Katie Brown was a famous climber who turned pro when she was like 14. I also knew that the move I had done wasn't very hard, but it was kind of fun to hear it.

I didn't climb much more that day. I watched the guys for a little bit and they didn't pay too much attention to me. Riding back to town was awesome. For one thing, I knew where I was going and knew I wouldn't accidentally wander into Strider's camp. But mostly, the trail sloped gradually down and had a number of gently arching curves and no really sharp turns. I could go really fast. I worried a little about slamming into someone coming up the hill, but it was late and I didn't really expect anyone to be riding up into the woods now. I zipped through the orchard and back through town. I pulled into our neighborhood just as the streetlights were coming on. That had always been my bike riding curfew. Now, of course, I was the first one home. The house was empty and no one would have noticed if I had stayed out another hour.

CHAPTER 4: THE ANNIVERSARY

I managed to ride out to the Ravine a couple of times a week while Dad was in rehab. I visited him Saturdays, and generally got out to the Ravine on Sundays. Dad made a lot of progress in rehab. He got so that he could sit up without throwing up. Everybody was so excited about that. Give me a break. This was a guy who could do pushups with me sitting on his back. He could mountain bike with his buddies all morning and still blow me off the trail in the afternoon. He carried most of my gear when we went backpacking and talked all the way up the steepest hills without sounding short of breath. And now, we were supposed to get excited because he could sit up without puking. Then came other thrilling accomplishments. He could roll a wheelchair. He learned to transfer from the wheelchair to the bed with the help of only one person. Gotta be thrilled with that. The rehab staff seemed to care most about his toilet issues and his skin. I don't think they had any idea who the man in that skin really was. So, you can probably tell that I didn't hang around in rehab a whole lot. Mom came home every night and told us that Dad "loved" rehab. He was really "getting into it" and was making great progress and impressing the staff. Yeah right, these were people who were impressed if you didn't puke on them when they sat you up. Rolling over in bed made you a superstar. Go Dad.

Unfortunately, things didn't change a whole lot when Dad got home. Sure, there was somebody in the house now, but in addition to Dad, there was usually a home health therapist doing exercises with him. Mom cut back to working half time. She spent a couple of hours with Dad and his "morning routine," then worked for about four hours and came back to help him again in the evening. Dad was too busy to hang out so I kept taking my bike rides after school. The Ravine sort of became my special place. There I could forget about Dad's injury and all the changes at home, and just climb. From the first day, when that guy called me Katie Brown, everybody at the Ravine knew me as Katie. I don't think any of them know my name.

Over time, I got pretty good at the main traverse. That's the most popular, long sideways climb at the Ravine. At first, I could make a move here and there, but couldn't put any of them together. Some nights I'd go to the rock, warm up, and then just try one move over and over again. Each time I'd lean a little bit differently or put my foot in a slightly different position to adjust my balance. It was amazing. Sometimes I'd try a move fifty times over the course of several weeks before I'd finally be able to get it. Then, once I had it, I could make it every time, like it was easy. Climbers say they have a hard move "wired" when it gets easy.

Eventually, I pretty much wired the whole traverse and started working on variations. The guys got used to me and hardly seemed to notice me. Once in a while one of them would spot me if I went high. Rarely, they'd be swearing and talking about some girl they knew and one of them would hush them and point at me (like he thought they shouldn't talk like that in front of a little girl). But mostly, they didn't seem to care if I was there or not.

I thought I'd go crazy when winter came and I couldn't make it out to the Ravine very often. I was forced to spend more time in the house. By that time, Dad was done with home health and was going to physical therapy at a clinic three times a week. Mom was back to working full time and Walter was consumed with the whole High School experience. Christmas was awkward. Relatives came to visit since we weren't traveling anywhere. Christmas shopping for Dad was a challenge. What do you get for a guy who spends most of his time in physical therapy or at home in a wheelchair? I got him a little pack that could hook onto the side of his chair. I was starting to get impatient for him to get out and start living again. I thought he could put a cell phone and a water battle, snack etcetera, into the bag and get out and about. I knew he couldn't go skiing or rock climbing, but I thought he should get outside at least. He wasn't dead. He could get out to some of the places he had always loved. But my gift was put to a different use.

Dad's work buddies took over Christmas morning with their incredibly stupid gift. Dad was some kind of water safety engineer. He worked for the city at the water treatment plant. He really seemed to like the guys he worked with, even though they never really did stuff together outside of work. I think his coworkers were beer, bar, and bowling guys. Dad was Mr. outdoor sports -- mountain biking, backpacking, skiing, climbing. Sports that didn't need a team and weren't big on TV. Sports you could do your whole life, not just in high school. That is, unless a drunk ran over you and put you in a wheelchair. Well, Dad's work friends must have thought he'd become one of them now. They visited a lot after his injury. They invited him to come watch them bowl. No really, *watch them bowl*. How lame did they think he was. He broke his back. He didn't lose his brain. Anyway, on Christmas morning the guys delivered their present. They looked like they had just discovered pizza or something really impressive. They blew in and set up a new, giant, wide screen television. The first thing Walter did was to put the remote into the pack I gave Dad. Not sunscreen, a GPS, compass or bug spray, a freakin' TV remote in the bag I gave Dad. Clearly, everybody else was content to let Dad sit inside and watch other people have fun on TV. The only thing that saved Christmas for me was the indoor climbing gym membership that Mom gave me. I didn't have to sit at home and watch Dad watch TV. I could go to the gym after school and on weekends and climb. It kept me sane until Spring.

Winter hung on forever that year. I looked forward to the snow melting, hoping that Dad would start to go out more. Maybe try some trails. I also missed the Ravine and climbing on real rock. Every time the snow melted; we got another storm. Finally, we had a warm week and most of the snow melted in town. The weekend was sunny and almost felt more like summer than spring. By Sunday, I could no longer hold myself back, I hopped on my bike and pedaled out towards the Ravine. I made it through the orchard, over the whoops, and started up the trail into the woods before hitting a snow drift across the trail. I pedaled hard into the snow. The harder I pedaled, the slower I went until my bike stuck firmly in the drift. I hopped off and stood beside the entrenched bike. The snow was hard-packed and icy. My sneakers slipped and slid, but didn't sink much. I lifted the bike and dragged it out of the ruts and across the drift. The trail was clear for a few yards, but I sunk into the next drift and the one after that. From there, the trail vanished into a field of snow. There were no footprints or bike tracks. There were some very old ski tracks, but nothing recent. I wondered where Strider stayed in the winter. Clearly, he wasn't biking up and down this hill. I wondered if he came back to the same place every summer or if he moved his camp around.

Thoroughly defeated, I turned and dragged my bike back through the drifts. Snow, slush and dirt flew off the tires as I rode back down through the whoops. The Ravine would have to wait a few more weeks. Back in town, I wondered at the difference in weather. It was so sunny and warm and the grass was green. Well, greenish since it was really uncovered for the first time since winter, but way more green than the snow-covered woods I had just left. I went to the climbing gym and worked on a couple of boulder problems I was really sick of.

Spring totally failed me. When the rain and cold finally stopped, summer was in full burn. Hot and sweaty summer with no transition from the winter. I was glad to get back to the Ravine, but it was hot, buggy, and slimy from sweat. I guess I was a little soft from climbing indoors all winter. As much as I loved it, I didn't get out to the Ravine as often as I had expected. The same guys were often there, and they still called me Katie Brown. Towards the end of summer we had a few weeks of cooler, dry weather, and I finally hit the groove with my climbing. I got out to the Ravine several days a week. My climbing improved and so did my biking from all the rides out there.

That stretch at the end of summer was the best time I had since Dad's accident. Walter was back in football with two-a-day practices, so he wasn't around to irritate me. Mom and Dad were busy with their stuff, and I was climbing my brains out. So, it made no sense to me when it all fell apart after a few weeks. None of the good things changed, but I started to feel terrible. I had trouble getting up in the mornings, I lost my appetite and I started to get really anxious on my bike rides to the edge of town. The only time I felt okay was at the Ravine, but I even had trouble getting myself there. Mom had been trying to get me to see a psychologist ever since Dad's injury. She and Dad met with one at the rehab center a few times. I never made it. I was pretty sure that telling some stranger about my dad's injury was not going to help anything; especially some stranger who obviously already knew all about the injury because she had been talking with Dad. Still, every time I got a little upset or sad, Mom pulled out the old psychologist referral. She made no sense. Any time I showed any feelings, she suggested I go talk about my feelings. If my feelings were so important, how come she freaked out every time I showed some. If I wasn't allowed to talk about my feelings with my family, why would I want to take them to a stranger. Obviously, I didn't go see the shrink. Neither did Walter, so I was really surprised when Dad mentioned her at dinner one night.

"Dr. Benton asked if I had been thinking about the anniversary. She said that it might be useful to talk about it, or plan to do something together on that day."

This made no sense at all to me. The only anniversary I had ever heard of was Mom and Dad's wedding anniversary. That was in June and I was quite certain that we did something together. We went out to a restaurant or something. What other anniversary did we have to talk about?

Dad went on, "You know, I had been thinking some about it. Mostly this week, cuz last year this week had been so fun. Remember our end of summer CBC week Kelly?"

I was blown away. Remember my best week ever? Duh. Best week ever followed by worst day, worst week, worst month, and worst year. I was just thinking "worst life" when the "year" thing rang in my head.

"One year since your injury," I said.

Everybody at the table looked at me like I had just come back from one of my space outs.

"Yeah," said Dad. "I know it's not a celebration kind of anniversary, but Dr. Benton said that it's important to acknowledge the year because people generally have some kind of a reaction, and it can go a lot better if they do it consciously."

Whatever. So, his injury ruined the best week of my life last year, and now it was trashing the best time I had since the accident. Nice.

While I was ranting in my head, the rest of the family decided that we would acknowledge the anniversary date with a meal together at home and would share some of our feelings about how things had changed and what things we were grateful for. When we left the table, Walter bumped me in the shoulder and muttered, "Don't freak out on us at the anniversary." He's the freak.

The anniversary wasn't too bad. We rarely ate together anymore, because of Walter's football and Mom's work schedule. But at the anniversary dinner, we seemed more like a family than we had in a long time. We didn't talk much about feelings. Everybody was glad Dad was alive and back home. Mom was thankful for her flexible job. Then, somehow, we ended up talking about Walter's upcoming football game.

After the anniversary, I did start to feel a little better and got in some good climbing days before school started.

Mom was there to tape us on the first morning of school. Dad was home, but he hadn't made it up and out of his room yet. I was returning to middle school and Walter was starting his sophomore year in high school, so there were no big changes, and it was easy to get back into the swing of things.

A few weeks into the school year, I stepped out of the school and saw Dad rolling up from the parking lot. My friend Sierra sort of squealed and ran to meet him.

What a freak, I thought. She acted like Dad was cool just because he was in a wheelchair.

Over by the stairs, a group of popular girls was holding coolness court with Princess Phoebe. She and three of her bitch friends looked from Dad to me and whispered. They thought Dad was just gross because he was paralyzed.

I just wanted him to be Dad, not paralyzed Dad, or wheelchair Dad. Certainly not TV-watching Dad. But the new year hadn't brought back any of his old activity. He still seemed to think that if you were in a wheelchair, you were supposed to just watch life instead of living it. He acted like sitting in a wheelchair watching TV was a "new normal" for him. I wanted to shake him and say, "Dad, you can't walk. You can't get up from a chair. You can't go to the bathroom. Things are not normal and you can't let them stay this way!"

But I didn't. I also didn't actually run around calling my friends freaks and swearing at the popular girls. Obviously, it wouldn't be right for a girl whose dad had been paralyzed to swear or cause trouble or complain. After all, look what he was going through. I was supposed to make things easy for him; to be a "good girl". Of course, it was okay for all the other twelve-year-old girls to go a little nuts. Their parents just rolled their eyes and said, "Well, she's at that age." I missed eleven because of his injury. Now it looked like twelve would be ruined by his recovery. I was not pleased.

"Hi Dad," I said. "You know, I rode my bike today. You didn't have to come pick me up."

"Yeah Babe, I was just going to Walter's practice and I thought you might want to come hang out with me. We could throw your bike in the back of the truck."

It's amazing how much things had changed since Dad's accident. A year ago Walter was just an average boy with an old man's name. After Dad got hurt, Walter decided he was the reincarnation of Walter Payton (some football player who used to be famous), and everyone started acting like football was important. Dad always encouraged us to do our own things, but he didn't make too much of team sports. Walter used to bike and ski and climb with us. Or, sometimes, we would drop Walter off at football practice and go rock climbing or hiking. Wheelchair Dad just wanted to sit and watch football. Okay, so he couldn't really rock climb anymore. At least he could get out and hike (or roll) down a trail.

"That sounds great Dad," I finally answered, "but I was planning to go by Jennifer's on the way home. Maybe I can go to practice with you tomorrow."

"Okay. Mom is working late and there will be a scrimmage at practice tonight, so we won't all be back for supper. If you're the first one home, there is some leftover pizza in the fridge you can heat up."

"Okay Dad, I'll see you tonight."

"Love ya babe," said Dad as he spun back to the parking lot.

"Your dad is so cool. He's so brave to be out on his own in that wheelchair."

"Goodbye Sierra."

I watched Dad roll out to his truck. He opened the passenger door, slid in and then pulled the chair up behind him. He folded it as he lifted it and slid across the seat to the driver's side. Then he leaned back over the chair and closed the door. He had his truck modified after his injury so he could drive with hand controls. As he pulled into the street and drove by the front of the administration building, he honked and waved at Phoebe and her gang. I had to smile. The last thing she wanted was some gimp waving at her. I watched her wave back and turn away quickly.

I certainly didn't want to hang out here. Walking back into the school, I grabbed my backpack from my locker. Then I stopped in the bathroom. I had been having stomach cramps all day but still couldn't go. I was on my way out to the woods and the last thing I wanted was to have to go out there. I have gotten pretty good at peeing in the woods, but I'd still rather not have to poop out there. I pulled out the water bottle, filled it at the fountain, and munched on an apple. In the schoolyard, I put the bottle on my bike and finished my apple as I re-locked the bike lock onto the rack. This was my favorite time of day. Leaving school and heading out on my bike. My own time. My best time.

I hopped off the curb and headed toward Jennifer's house. She wouldn't see me zip by her house because she was at soccer practice. Okay, I didn't feel good about it, but it wasn't a total lie. I did say I would "go by" Jennifer's house. I didn't actually say I was going to stay there. I still hadn't told my parents that I was spending time at the Ravine. I didn't want them to worry. Or, worse yet, to say I couldn't go.

Just past Jennifer's house I hit the apple orchard. I dropped into the gully picking up as much speed as I could handle to propel me up the slope on the other side. Then I shifted down and steadily plugged up the hill. Like everything else, shifting reminded me of my dad. He bugged me non-stop when I was learning to ride, trying to get me to shift. For a while, I wouldn't even ride with him because it annoyed me so much. Then, when I rode on my own, I started to learn how much it helped. Now when I ride with my friends, I can hardly keep from yelling at them to shift their stupid gears.

I couldn't wait to get to the Ravine because I was planning to complete a new problem that I had never seen anyone else do.

Several times in the past two weeks, I had had the Ravine to myself and I had started working on a new ending to the main traverse. At the far left edge of the Ravine, the rock ended and became overhanging at the top. To finish the traverse you had to pull up two big hard moves that the guys called the *Urban Guerilla*. Those last two moves had taken me all summer to learn. After pulling the *Urban Guerilla*, you could take a step to the left and move onto a trail that came up the left side of the Ravine. Once I had those moves wired, I started to look for another finish. When no one was around, I explored a lower route that stayed really close to the ground at the overhang and then pulled up at the very furthest left edge of the rock. The moves leaned way out backwards, and the handholds were tiny and dirty and very difficult. I worked it for a few days and almost made the moves the last time I tried. Now, two days later, I was confident I could make it. Whoever does a climb first gets to name it and I was thinking I would call it *The Lowdown*. It would be the first problem I ever put up myself.

CHAPTER 5: FIRSTS

I rode up to the spot where the trail branched off to Strider's camp. I leaned my bike against a tree and grabbed an energy bar out of my pack. I quickly and quietly ran up the trail to the tree that lay across the path. I set the bar on the tree and ran back to my bike. I jumped on and pedaled away. This had become a tradition for me. But still, after probably 20 or 30 times, my heart still pounds when I run up there. I've never seen him again in the woods, and I hope I don't. But for some reason I keep leaving him an energy bar. I guess I was so scared the first time, and I feel like I'm riding through his yard now since I know where he camps so I leave him an homage or a toll for using his backyard. Sometimes I think I'm brave to run up there and nice to leave him a bar. Other times, I think I'm just a big old wuss for getting scared and for thinking I have to leave him gifts. I have no idea what he thinks, when I first returned this summer, I wasn't even sure he had come back to the same camp. He must have though, because the bars were always gone when I came back with a new one.

Finally, I finished the ride and rolled down the last stretch into the Ravine. The last drop into the Ravine is really steep and rocky. The first few times I walked my bike down. Eventually, I started trying to ride it. I had to move my butt back all the way behind the seat and stay really, really low to keep from flipping over the top. I practically lock up both brakes to keep from flying down the slope. I still don't always make it. Often, I hit a rock or a root and fall to the side, or the bike gets going too fast and I hop off the back and let it go crash by itself. This day, I was so pumped about the new boulder problem that I rode my bike all the way down into the Ravine like I had it wired. I leaned my bike on a bush and sat down on a rock with my pack. I still had some stomach cramps, so I took a little time to sip some water while I checked out the other climbers. There were three of the regular guys there. Two of them were working on a reach problem in the middle of the traverse. The other was sitting by his pack staring into space. I put away my water and pulled my climbing shoes out of my pack. I laced them up tightly then did a few of the easier moves on the traverse to warm up. The guys had looked over when I first showed up and one said, "hey" when he recognized me, but they kept working on their own stuff.

After I warmed up, I clipped on my chalk bag belt and opened the bright blue bag of chalk that hung down behind me. Just thinking about this climb made my hands sweat a little. I dipped my fingers into the bag and dusted them with chalk. The chalk dried my hands and helped my grip. It was time to try *The Lowdown*. I started near the end of the main traverse and worked my way over to *Urban Guerilla*. When I got there, I lowered myself as close to the ground as I could, bending my legs fully, leaning back, and squeezing my chest under the overhang. On most routes it helps to be tall and have a long reach, but on this problem, extra height would just make it more difficult. I'm a little tall for my age but shorter than any of the older guys who usually hang around here. I wondered if they would be able to pull this move even though they were much better climbers. But at this point, I couldn't look up to see if they were watching because I had to totally concentrate on the move. I squeezed left keeping my feet on some tiny edges close to the ground. I had just made it to the hardest part (the crux) when one of the guys yelled.

"Hey look, Katie Brown is doing *Squeeze Play*. I haven't seen anyone do that for a long time."

"Keep on it," another one said, "way left and level with your waist is the next hand hold. It sucks but it's all there is."

I knew this and didn't want someone to tell me. I had worked it out on my own after dozens of tries, and now they would think I made it because they had told me how. For a moment I was bummed and almost fell from staying in one place too long. Then I reminded myself that I really wanted to do this move and I slowly slid my left hand to the sucky hold then eased the rest of my body in that direction. When I got as far left as I could, I pulled myself in as close to the rock as I could get. Just as I started moving in, I let go with my right hand and reached up high for a little knob. I grabbed it just as my body started to swing back out from the rock. I squeezed that little knob for all I was worth and managed to stop my body from pulling me away from the rock. Next, I moved my feet up and grabbed a good hold with my left hand. Two more easy moves up and I could step off the rock and onto the trail.

"Nice job Katie Brown!" said one of the guys with more enthusiasm than they'd ever wasted on me before. I actually think they were a little impressed. Then of course, the same guy hopped on the route and cruised it like it was easy.

"Whoa," he said, "that's pretty tough Katie Brown. Nice climbing"

"Thanks," I answered. Yeah right, I thought. He had just made it look simple. However, the next guy who tried fell twice before he got it. The second time he fell he slammed his hand into the ground and cussed. His buddy looked at me and saw the big smile on my face and smiled back. I'm glad the guy that fell didn't see me. He probably would have thought that I was laughing at him. I wasn't. I was just really happy that I made it and that it didn't look too easy now. I was so pumped. Later, while the rest of us were climbing on other parts of the rock, I saw the third guy try it. He never really got close, but I could tell he was studying it and would be back to get it soon. *Squeeze Play*, what a stupid name. I can't believe someone had already climbed it and named it. I had never seen anyone on those moves and two weeks ago, when I started working them, they were coated with dirt. I had never named a route. I guess *The Lowdown* will have to wait.

I messed around on a couple more moves but then my cramps got worse and I sat back down to sip some water and change out of my climbing shoes. That's when I noticed it. There was a little blood on my thigh right at the edge of my shorts. At first I thought I must have scratched myself climbing. But there was no scratch. Then I realized that my underwear was damp. I had thought it was just sweat.

Oh crap, I thought. What a place and time to start my first period. The cramps, the blood. I was twelve. Some of my friends had started. I knew it was coming but I was not ready. I must have turned pale. One of the climbers actually looked over and asked me if I was all right. How could it get more humiliating? I guess I should be glad he didn't notice me bleeding. Okay, I had to get out of there. I wiped my leg with my shorts and grabbed my pack. I pushed my bike up the hill and then hopped on and pedaled a little ways down the trail. I found a place to pull off the trail and stepped back into the trees with my pack. My pack was well stocked. There was an emergency whistle, waterproof matches and a little space blanket. I had energy bars and a little first aid kit, my water bottle and some toilet paper folded up in a zip lock bag. No pads. I know a girl at school who has been carrying pads in her purse since she was 10 just in case. I thought she was ridiculous, but I sure could use one now. I pulled some of the toilet paper out of the baggie, folded it up and put it in my underwear. I suddenly felt exhausted and sick. I sat on a rock and stared at my bike. I wiped my eyes and notice the tears. "Oh crap, now I'm turning into a girlie girl." I couldn't believe it was happening just like that.

I wasn't the biggest tomboy around, but I liked to do a lot of stuff. Before my dad got hurt, Walter and I used to do everything with him. We climbed and mountain biked and backpacked. We would hike out to little lakes in the mountains and go swimming naked. Mom rarely came with us. It seemed she was always on her period. Sometimes she said she couldn't get too far from a bathroom, or she worried that the cold water in the lake would make her "flow too much." We did a lot of fun stuff with her too, but the real physical stuff was always me and the guys. I didn't want that to end. I didn't want to learn to knit and stay home and cook. I felt more tears falling. I didn't want to cry either. This really sucked.

I tried to remember all the TV commercials for "feminine products." Girls skiing and swimming. Girls wearing all white. Damn, I hope those products work. I had to find a way to handle this. I also had to get home before the toilet paper in my shorts got soaked. I got back on my bike and pedaled home.

Just as I had expected, I was the first one home. I went to Mom and Dad's bathroom and found a pad. I hoped Mom would get home first so I could talk with her about this. I hated being in their bathroom since Dad's injury. He had a shower chair, and rails by the toilet. I knew things about his bathroom habits that daughters should not have to think about. He had to give himself a suppository every morning to make him poop. They call it his "bowel program." I learned about that when he was finishing inpatient rehab. Since then, I tried to stay away whenever he started talking about his injury. Mom and Walter could listen, but I already had too much information.

When he first came home from rehab, his morning routine took about 2 hours. He needed help with everything. My poor mom had to help with all that stuff too. I don't know how they did it. Now he can do everything by himself, and I think it takes a lot less time. He is usually getting up when we leave for school, but he often comes by the school in the morning when he goes downtown for coffee, so I know he gets going pretty quickly.

I went out to the kitchen and nuked a piece of pizza. I was supposed to be reading a book for a school report. I looked at the mail, petted the cat and looked around for something else to delay my homework. Finally, I went to my room and put on a CD. Just as I lay down on my bed to read, they all came home. Apparently, Mom had gone by Walter's practice. Unbelievable. It was just a freakin' practice! The boys went right to the kitchen to get food, so I followed Mom back to her bedroom. She was pretty distracted. She asked me about my day while she was changing clothes but kept on changing and didn't appear to expect an answer. After a while I said, "I started my period."

That got her attention. She stopped with her sweater over her head and let out some kind of a funny scream sound. When her head emerged from her sweater, she looked like I'd just told her I won the Nobel prize or something. She was so excited. I couldn't help but smile too. I didn't really understand why she thought this was so great. It's not like I had done anything, it just happened. And, we both knew it was going to happen. Still, it was really fun seeing her get so psyched. She grabbed me and gave me a big hug. There were actually tears in her eyes. Then, suddenly, she pushed me away and said, "Oh my gosh, we should get you something." She looked at my crotch as if she expected to see blood running down my leg.

"I already got one of your pads Mom," I told her.

"Oh good, do you know how to use it?"

"It's not exactly rocket science," I said, "I just pulled off the paper and stuck it to my vagina."

"No!" she screamed, "You stick it to your panties."

"Mom!" I said. "Duh!"

"Oh, I'm sorry," she said. "Don't tease me. I'm just so excited. Did you tell Dad?"

"Mom, you all just walked in."

"Okay, yeah, alright. This is so great. Are you alright?"

"I'm fine Mom."

"Hey, let's go out for dinner. Have you eaten?"

"I had some pizza, and I have homework."

"Okay, how about lunch tomorrow? I could pick you up at school. No, wait, I have a lunch meeting. How about dinner tomorrow?"

"Walter has a game".

"Okay, then this weekend. We'll go out to lunch and do some shopping. Just the two of us."

"Okay Mom, that'll be great"

Dad came in about then, and Mom had me tell him.

"Oh great" he said, "now I've got to put up with two women in the house." But he was smiling really big when he said it. He looked like he wanted to give me a hug but that's not so easy when you're in a chair, so he just took my hand in his for a second and looked into my eyes. I love it when he does that.

"Hey Joan, we have another woman in the family...." Mom was already on the phone calling her sister. Great, what would she do next? Put a big sign in our front yard: "It's a Period!"

I headed out to the living room. I really didn't want to hear the details of Mom's phone call with Aunt Joan. For once, Walter's cluelessness was an advantage. He was sitting in front of the TV eating cold pizza and watching sports news. Blood could have been running out of my eyes and he wouldn't have noticed. I watched as he finished the pizza and automatically reached down to pick up a football. It wasn't there. He looked around the room and saw it lying by my feet. He looked like a little baby that couldn't reach its pacifier.

"Toss me that ball," he said without looking up at me. I waited for a minute and watched him start to squirm. "Come on," he said, "I can't get comfortable without something in my hands."

What a freak. I tossed the football into his lap. It was true. He was usually sitting in front of the TV with either food or a ball in his hands. I watched him twirl the ball on his finger and then toss it from hand to hand. He was just a big kid. This was interesting. I started my period. Everyone is saying I've become a woman and look at my big brother. No one is saying "you're a man now" to him. He's two years older than me, and he's just a big old boy while I'm becoming a woman. Perhaps there could be some advantage to this. After all, Mom was taking me shopping. I'd have to take over a drawer in the bathroom for pads and stuff. Walter would certainly leave that alone. The things I usually like to buy -- gear for my bike or for climbing, are always getting "borrowed" by Walter or Dad. Now I would collect some stuff that would be all my own. Definitely not used by Walter. Actually, that's not true. Walter once came home from wrestling practice with a piece of a tampon stuck up his nose. He said the trainers kept them just for bloody noses because they absorbed more than anything else. What a freak.

Dad rolled in to watch TV. He kept looking up at me with some strange expression, like he was about to say something or maybe laugh. After about the third time I told him to stop it and went to my room to read my book.

CHAPTER 6: OH BROTHER

School was a bit awkward the next day. I had to drag my whole backpack into the bathroom with me every time I went. So this is how it happens; one day of menstruating and I'm thinking about buying my first purse. I had to find something smaller than that pack. I only told Sierra. I knew she had gotten her period last year.

"Welcome to the club," she said. "It only sucks a little. Did your mom cry?"

"Yeah" I said, "what's up with that?"

"I have no idea. But worse than that, my dad acted like I was contagious for about a month. He practically avoided me."

"My dad was cool" I said. But I began to wonder. We had already stopped hanging out since his injury. I wondered if this was the final straw; if we'd start to act like those father/daughter pairs who don't seem to know each other at all. I couldn't handle that. I guess I was in a pretty sucky mood for the rest of the day. That was probably part of the reason for my problems at Walter's game that night.

It was the first game of the season. Walter went straight from school. Mom finally came home from work at a decent time, but they were both rushing around to get ready for the game. Dad had been to some practices at the school field, but this would be his first time to the actual stadium in a wheelchair and he didn't know what to expect. He had a pack on his wheelchair loaded with catheters and assorted bathroom stuff. He added binoculars and piled on enough clothes for a winter game (it was that late summer weather of hot days and really cool nights). He was not looking forward to using the restroom in the stadium. He went into way too much detail describing the typical state of mens' rooms in stadiums. From the sound of it, men walk in the door and start to spit and piss on the floor on their way to the urinals. Actually, he said they don't even have urinals, just some kind of trough along one wall. He said guys pee in the general direction of the trough wall, never put a toilet seat up when they pee in the toilet and generally act like farm animals in a pig sty. Apparently, he didn't mind when he could join them. But now that he had to roll through the room and sit on a toilet, he was a bit more judgmental.

We had a quick supper then loaded into the van. That's another thing that changed. I don't think I ever saw my dad in a passenger seat before his injury. Now he drives his own truck, but Mom always drives when we take the van. Dad transferred into the passenger seat, and I rolled his chair around to the back of the van. Their conversation on the way to the game was interesting. Through summer practices and the preseason, they had been so excited about Walter's football that you would have thought he was the starting quarterback. Now they wondered aloud whether he would even get in the game. He is a sophomore and this was his first year on the varsity team (ninth grade had their own team). He played linebacker but wasn't a starter. He was on the kicking teams and would get to play on the kickoffs and punts. Dad said he was quick and smart but a little small for linebacker. Unless someone got injured or our team got way ahead (or behind), we might not even see Walter much.

We used the handicap parking right beside the stadium. Our high school has an old stadium that isn't all that accessible from a wheelchair. The ramps up to the seats were pretty steep. I helped push Dad and it was no small feat. Then, we learned that there wasn't any real wheelchair seating. I figured there would be some place where the seats were removed and you could park a wheelchair beside the regular seats. I walked from one end of the stadium to the other and found no such place. Dad was about to roll back down the ramp to ask at the ticket booth, but I told him I would go. He and Mom were at the top of the ramp watching Walter in warm-ups when I headed down to the ticket office. I had to wait in a line to get to the ticket guy.

"Where is the wheelchair seating?" I asked.

"The what?"

"Where do people in wheelchairs go?" I tried again.

"I don't know" he said. "I just sell the tickets".

"Well, is there anyone here who would know?" I was not in a good mood, and I'm sure I was starting to sound bitchy.

"I guess I could call upstairs and ask someone," he said, but he didn't move.

"Will you please do that?"

"Yeah, fine. But listen, there is a line behind you. Can you move over to the side to wait. I'll call."

I should have said "no" and stayed there until he did something, but I stepped to the side and watched in frustration as he started selling tickets to the next people in line without making a call. I was so mad; at him and at myself for not doing anything. I just stood there fuming and feeling helpless. Then I started to cry. I'm not a big crier, but now I was starting to lose it. I searched my pockets for a Kleenex. My nose was running; I had tears running down my cheeks. I turned toward the side of the ticket booth so no one could see me and wiped my face on my sleeve. That's when I felt a hand on my shoulder. It was the vice-principal, Mr. Jenkins.

"Hey" he said, "Can I help?"

As I turned around, he handed me a hanky. I wiped my face better. I really needed to blow my nose but didn't figure I could blow my nose in his handkerchief and then hand it back to him. The thought of giving Mr. Jenkins a hanky I had just blown my nose in almost made me smile even though my eyes were still watering.

"I can't find a place for Dad to sit," I mumbled.

He seemed to think for a minute, then he asked, "Is your mom with him?"

I thought this was a really irrelevant question.

"Yes" I said.

He turned to his wife.

"Honey, do we still have the lawn chairs in the trunk from Hannah's soccer game?"

"I'll go get one," was her answer.

"As soon as your eyes dry up, we'll go get him and take him down on the field. He can sit to the side of the team bench, and Helen will bring a lawn chair so your mom can sit with him. Did you want to sit there too?"

He seemed to have had the whole plan ready to go.

"No," I said. "I'll sit in the stands with my friends. I wiped my eyes again and handed his hanky back. He kind of held my hand a little when he took his hanky. So this was the big disciplinarian that all the trouble-makers at school were so worried about. Well, I could see that he got right to the point. But he didn't seem like a bad guy. I stood looking at the ground for a couple of minutes. He might not be a bad guy, but I sure didn't have anything to talk with him about.

"Let's go get your folks," he said. "Helen will meet us on the field with a chair for your mom." We walked up the ramp to where Mom and Dad were still waiting. Dad looked back and saw us coming.

"Hey Bud," he said. This kind of confused me because he often calls Walter "Bud". But Mr. Jenkins didn't seem to mind (later I learned that his name was actually Bud).

"Hey Jeff, I was just talking to your daughter about the seating in this stadium. Sorry it's not very accessible. You know, back in the 50s when they built this monstrosity they figured people with disabilities would have the decency to stay home where the rest of us wouldn't have to look at them."

For a second, I couldn't really believe what I was hearing. I looked up at Mr. Jenkins who had a big smile on his face. Dad was laughing

"I never really could mind my manners Bud," he said.

"You know," said Mr. Jenkins. "We're working on a bond measure to build a new facility. I've been working with the architect and we will blend in the wheelchair seating so folks can sit with their families in the stands. I'm afraid you'll be off watching Walter in college games by the time that's a reality. The best we can do here is to get you a good place on the field. How about a spot at the end of the bench?"

"That would be fine," said Dad. They started back down the ramp. Helen was just coming back into the stadium with a lawn chair.

"I'll stay up here with some friends," I yelled. Dad stopped and turned his chair around so he could see me.

"Okay," he said. "We'll meet up with you after the game." I forced a weak smile.

I stayed at the rail and watched as they came out the side of the stands and headed to the edge of the field. The four of them went past the bench and set up a lawn chair beside Dad at the sideline. Then they stood around chatting like old friends. I hadn't even known that Dad had ever met Mr. Jenkins. Neither Walter nor I ever got into the kind of trouble that gets the parents called in to the vice principal's office. My gaze drifted down the sideline. There was Walter with a small group of players getting last minute instructions from one of the coaches. Right up beside the bench was another wheelchair. This one had a kid in it. Ty Ty Tyler. He was a fixture at all the games and practices. He always wore a school football jersey. I think he was about a year older than Walter. He had been in special ed classes at my school, but now he must be in some high school classes. His speech was really hard to understand, he stuttered a lot. He couldn't walk and he had poor control of his hands and arms. He always seemed to have food stuck on the front of his shirt. He laughed really loud when he was happy, and he was always happy when one of the football players noticed him. Walter said they had kind of adopted him. They helped him around the hallways, and he went to every practice and home game.

I looked from Ty Ty to Dad. Surely people wouldn't put them in the same category just because they were both in wheelchairs. I got even more worried about all the time Dad was spending at football games and practices. I couldn't let him turn in to a Ty Ty Tyler. I pictured the two of them sitting together in their wheelchairs at practices. I wanted to scream at Dad to get the hell out of there.

He was still talking with Mr. Jenkins. Then I remembered. I looked back at Ty Ty. Tyler was Mr. Jenkins' kid. That's how Dad knew Mr. Jenkins. They probably saw each other at the practices. I didn't know what to make of this. On the one hand, I didn't want Mr. Jenkins to treat my Dad like his disabled son. On the other hand, they appeared to be getting along like friends. Dad hadn't seen much of his friends the last few months. At first, in the weeks after the accident, they hung around all the time. But, when Dad didn't get back to work, they seemed to drop him. Not that I blamed them. He never went out or did anything and even those guys could get tired of talking about TV sports eventually. They were all continuing to hunt and fish and bowl and they never saw Dad anywhere unless they came to the house. It was probably good if he got to know Mr. Jenkins....Bud.

I turned to scan the stands to find some of my friends. I saw a group of younger girls. Hannah Jenkins was right in the middle of a loud, laughing bunch. I watched her telling some story with lots of hand motion and squealing. I looked back at her brother sitting in a wheelchair on the field. How could she be so happy? How could she have so much fun when her brother was sitting there in front of everyone drooling on himself? As I watched, the players filed by Ty Ty and each slapped his hand as they moved to the bench to get ready for the kickoff. Ty Ty was laughing the whole time. I glanced back to Dad. He was shaking hands with Bud as Bud and Helen headed back to the stands. Everybody seemed to be having a good time. Was this for real, or were they just play-acting? I sure wasn't enjoying this.

I don't know how long I stood there looking at the crowd. Suddenly, I realized that the game was starting. Walter doesn't get to play much, but he is on the kickoff coverage team. He was super psyched when the coach put together the special teams and put a bunch of the sophomores on kickoff and punt coverage. He figured if he could make some great plays on special teams, then he would get in more often at linebacker. I hurried to the base of the stands and then turned to watch the kickoff. Walter was the second player from the end on the near side of the field. The kickoff went deep to the other side. Walter went flying down the field. He didn't run towards the ball but ran pretty much straight up the field. I watched as the player on the other team caught the kick and sprinted straight up the field. On our side, Walter eluded a block and kept moving up field. On the other side a couple of his teammates got blocked and the guy with the ball blasted straight up the field. By the time Walter looked over and saw the guy with the ball on the other side, it was all over. Walter turned to cross the field but was miles behind as the guy ran it into the end zone. The visitors' stands went crazy.

Walter ran back to the bench towards a screaming coach. I bet he rather would have faced every screaming fan on the other side. The coach waved all the sophomores over to one end of the bench. He quickly picked out five other players and assigned positions to them. When the teams went back out for the following kickoff, the sophomores stayed by the bench. Most of them took off their helmets and sat down. Walter stayed right on the edge of the sideline, still wearing his helmet. He was practically vibrating, sort of bouncing up and down real quickly. He watched the kickoff, which his team returned about six yards, and he continued to stand and bounce for the next few plays. They had to punt, and he bounced over by the coach and looked up expectantly. From where I stood, I could see the coach was avoiding Walter's gaze. The upper classmen went back in for the punt and the guy who caught it was tackled right away. The coach yelled praise and almost knocked Walter down as he turned to walk up field. Walter followed along. He yelled support to the linebackers on the first series. The other team got a first down but was stopped a few plays later. No sophomores went out on the punt return team. I turned to find some friends in the stands.

Sierra waved, and I climbed up to where she and several others were sitting.

"I saw your dad!" Sierra said, as if she had spotted a celebrity. "I bet he's got a great view from right there on the sideline."

I ignored her and sat down. Walter continued to stand and vibrate the entire first half. He came out of the locker room after half-time with his helmet off but continued standing on the side-line. Often, he was as close to the coach as he could get. I wasn't sure that was a good strategy. The coach was starting to look really annoyed when Walter didn't get out of his way fast enough.

We ended up winning by 14 points. I really thought he might put Walter back in near the end. Walter looked stunned when time ran out. Maybe he didn't know that it was the fourth quarter and thought there would still be time to play. He kept staring at the scoreboard and the 00:00. For the first time in the game, he sat down on the bench. I've never seen such a pathetic sight.

I looked over to Dad. He had started to wheel back across the track towards the stands. I was glad he didn't see Walter. Walter looked like he hardly had enough energy to drag himself in to the locker room. I ran down to the front of the stands where the players entered the locker room. People were yelling congratulations to the team. I wanted to say something to help Walter but all I could think of was "nice play". Just in time, I realized that that sounded really sarcastic and kept my mouth shut. I was watching him follow the team into the locker room when someone put a hand on my shoulder. I looked up to see Mom.

"Dad went on out to the car," she said. "Are you ready to go?"

I looked around to see my friends wandering off in small groups or with their parents. I hooked Mom's arm and started toward the parking lot. We didn't talk on the walk to the car. Mom and I didn't see a lot of each other these days and that actually made it harder to have stuff to talk about. It was like she lived in her work world, and I was some other place. Who knows what that place was. I wasn't really into school. I did my work but spent a lot of time spacing out. I have a few friends, but other than an occasional movie, we don't spend a lot of time together. Home is kind of a freak show lately. The only time I'm really focused is on my bike or on the rock. I wished I could share my climbing with someone.

Just as I was thinking that we came up on the van. Dad was transferring into the passenger seat. He had to pull himself up from his wheelchair to the seat. When he was first learning that move in rehab, it looked really hard. I remember him joking and saying that it was a "5.9" move. That's a rating for how difficult a climb is. Now he had it wired and made it look like a "5.3".

On the ride home, Mom and Dad talked about the game and Walter's one play. They knew he would be bummed about not playing more. Dad said that the coaches wouldn't blame Walter when they looked at the film and that he would probably get more playing time in future games.

When we got home Dad grabbed some food out of the refrigerator, and we snacked. Then, Mom and Dad went to their room. I heard their TV come on and I figured they were gone for the night. Mom would probably come out in a couple of hours to turn out all the lights and lock the doors. That used to be Dad's job too.

I read a little bit then went out on the porch. It was a really nice, cool, dark night. I watched as lights gradually went off in the houses up and down the street. Eventually, Walter came walking down the street, practically dragging his backpack. He was obviously still really bummed. I expected him to walk right past me without even acknowledging my existence. Instead, he plopped right down beside me without even acknowledging my existence. We sat in silence for quite a while. I tried to think of the right thing to say, but finally gave up.

"Are you alright?" I asked.

"Yup."

"I think Dad enjoyed being at the game," I tried.

"Did you give him another lecture about how he needs to get out more?"

"What are you talking about?"

"You know. You are always on his case for watching TV or reading. Why are you so mad at him? Why don't you just give him a break?"

I was completely taken by surprise. I expected Walter to be in a bad mood, but I didn't think he'd make up reasons to be mad at me. I just stared at him for a while. Maybe he'd come to his senses.

"You know it's true," he continued. "Ever since his accident, you've been on some kind of rampage. You either avoid us all or you jump on Dad's case. You're like chair flippin' angry all the time. Dad can't do anything to please you."

"I have not been 'on his case'. And what are you doing? Suddenly football is the most important thing in the world so Dad has something to watch while he sits on his butt?"

"There you go again. You do know that he can't walk don't you?"

"So he can't walk. That doesn't mean he can't get out and do stuff. You know what I mean. I know you miss it too. I just wish he would try."

"I think you have to adjust your expectations. Find new stuff to do with him. Football wasn't ever that important to him, but it is something he can be involved in. You have to find those kinds of things."

"If you weren't making such a big deal out of football, maybe he would make more of an effort to do other stuff."

Walter didn't get mad this time. He just sat there thinking.

"You know," he said after a while. "Dad did more goofy stuff with us than any other parent I know of. Remember his goofiest dive contest at the swimming pool?"

I smiled. "At first I just wanted to die with embarrassment, but my friends all got into it. By the end of the day we were all covered with red marks from slapping the water with our goofy dives. He really didn't mind looking like a dork."

"Didn't mind? He reveled in it! How about 'middle management man'? Whenever he was talking about his job he would put his hands on his hips and puff out his chest and say 'I am Middle Management Man'. He took dorkiness to new levels."

"Oh man, I remember the first day he came to my new middle school. You know, everybody at our old grade-school was used to him. When I started middle school, I was really worried about looking cool (or at least, halfway normal). I did okay for about two days. Then Dad got off early and decided to drop by just as school got out. He came riding up to the bike rack in his work cloths. He had a big old band wrapped around his pants leg, and he was wearing that home-made helmet cover we always hated. He got off his bike and started talking to some eighth-grade boys about their bikes. He kept his helmet on. There he was, walking around in that goofy helmet with his pants leg wrapped up, talking with a bunch of boys right by my bike. I was seriously thinking about leaving my bike and walking home just so I didn't have to walk over there. I thought those guys would give me so much crap, but they never said anything. How does he get away with that stuff?"

I don't think we had made fun of Dad since his injury. It didn't seem right to make fun of someone in a wheelchair. Now the memories and the laughter just came rolling out.

"Once, when I called him a Dork he said, '...and proud of it.' He said that being a dork was only a bad thing if you tried to deny it. If you embraced your dorkiness and took pride in it, it could be a powerful asset."

"He really is a dork isn't he?" said Walter.

"He set the standard high for the rest of us." I smiled. "I'm sorry you didn't get to play much in the game today."

"Oh well, I guess it's my fault. I did what the coach told me.

'Run straight up the field and contain the return man.' Yeah right. Next time I tackle the return man no matter where he is. I don't think I can take another entire game sitting on the bench."

I laughed at him. "What bench? You never sat down the entire game. A couple of times I thought you were going to tackle the coach."

"I need food," he answered, and we went in and sat on the kitchen counters while he ate about a meal and a half.

It felt good to hang with Walter again. We really hadn't talked much in the last year. In fact, he had a point. I hadn't had a good talk with anyone in the family for a long time.

CHAPTER 7: THE BIKE SHOP

The next morning when Mom and I got back from shopping I didn't even comment about Walter and Dad watching football on TV. I just told them I was going for a bike ride and headed out to the garage. I still had my climbing shoes in my pack and I had refilled my water bottle. I went to the storage shelves in the garage to get some more chalk for my chalk bag. I dug through the piles of Dad's climbing gear. Each piece brought back memories of things I had done with Dad. My first climbs, backpacking trips. I stood holding his old chalkbag and got lost in memories. Suddenly the garage door swung open. Mom came in to get some gardening tools. Luckily, her eyes took a while to adjust to the darker garage after being out in the sun, and she didn't see the tears streaming down my face. I quickly wiped my face on my t-shirt and grabbed some chalk from Dad's bag.

"Remember you need to be home by 4:00," Mom called as I rode away.

I was feeling good on the ride out. Shopping with Mom had been great. I still felt that Walter had been unfair in attacking me last night, but mostly, I felt such a relief from talking with him about Dad. Now it was a clear, cool day, and I was going to get in some climbing. As I rode, I thought about Walter's accusations. I didn't think I was mad at Dad. I know he didn't want to get injured, and he didn't do anything to cause it. I was mad at the drunk who hit him, but I'd already faced him. I wasn't mad at Dad for being paralyzed, I just wanted him to get on with life, to start doing more fun things instead of watching other people do them. I know I wanted to spend more time with Dad, but I wasn't going to spend it watching Walter practice football.

I dropped the energy bar on the stump by Strider's camp. In all the times I'd been out here, I'd never seen him again. I wonder if he has some kind of warning system that he can tell when people are around. The regular guys were at the Ravine when I arrived.

"Dang, I didn't know Katie Brown could mountain bike too," said one of the guys as I rode down the last steep slope to the rock. If he only knew how many times I had crashed or walked my bike down that death drop before I got it. I cruised *Squeeze Play* and worked on a couple of other problems. The cool sunny weather was perfect for climbing. It was a low gravity day for me; it seemed like gravity was less powerful, and I could hang on to little holds that were usually too small for me. It's amazing how strong you can be when you're in a good mood and the weather is fine. One of the older guys asked me for beta on *Squeeze Play*. I showed him the little side-pull that you needed to use to make the last move.

"Bummer," he said. "I saw that but hoped there was something better. You made it look way too easy."

That was pretty cool coming from one of the climber guys. Maybe I really was becoming a climber girl.

The ride home was great. I jammed down the hills as fast as I've ever ridden them, caught some air coming up into the orchard and then pretty much coasted back home. The garage door was open, and I was surprised to see Dad when I rolled in.

"Nice ride?" he asked. I must have been smiling.

"Yeah. What are you up to?"

"Now that I have a backup chair, I thought I'd tune this one up a bit."

He had gotten a wheelchair from his auto insurance company when he was in rehab. Recently, his health insurance company had agreed to buy him a chair also. He said he needed a different setup now that he had regained some strength in his stomach and chest muscles. He also wanted to set up one chair for going outdoors this winter and one for in the house. He was replacing a standard tire with a knobby Mt. bike tire.

"I never noticed that your wheels were so much like bike wheels."

"Yeah, actually, the chairs have a lot of bike components. All my bike tools should come in pretty handy". He popped the new tire on to the wheel and grabbed the pump. I helped hold the wheel while he pumped it up.

"Hey," I said. "While you're at it. I'm having trouble hitting the top gear on my bike."

He looked around the garage and motioned to the bike stand.

"Maybe if you dig out that stand, I could set your bike up where I could get at it."

I pulled out the work stand, and we cleared an area and mounted the bike. I was able to place it at a perfect level for him to reach the parts he wanted to adjust. He had his tool box on the floor. I found a small table and set it up within better reach for him.

"You know, these cables are in pretty bad shape. Maybe we should just replace them all. Would you want to work on that with me?"

I love that my dad works on bikes and can pretty much fix anything that happens to them. And, I love to be with my dad and to do stuff with him. However, I do not like to work on bikes with him. Either, he's really into it and I just have to stand around and hand him tools, or, he tries to show me how to do stuff that looks really easy for him and makes no sense at all to me. It's a no win situation. I'd have to be an idiot to say yes.

"Sure," I said. "That would be great!"

Okay, so it will suck for me. But, he will be working on bikes again, and I will be with him. How bad can it be?

52

"Do you want to start stripping off the old cable?"

"Oh no, I just remembered piano lessons" (Really, I did.)

"Oh well, I have to get some more cable anyway. Let's hit the bike shop tomorrow and work on this in the afternoon."

"Great," I said as I headed inside to clean up. I left him rearranging things in the garage to set up for working on my bike.

Sunday we went to the bike shop about noon. It was one of those cool, sunny fall days that has a special feel to it. The combination of bright sun and cool air makes all your senses sharp. The colors are brighter, the smells are more crisp. We rode in Dad's truck with the windows open and the radio on. Neighbors were working on their yards and kids were biking and skateboarding in driveways. It felt so "normal". I looked over at Dad sitting next to me. It was the first time I realized that, when he was driving, he looked like he did before his injury. When we pulled up to a car at a stoplight, the people would look in and see a dad and his daughter. Not a paralyzed dad or a paraplegic dad, or a poor crippled guy with his unfortunate daughter. They just saw a guy and his daughter. Odd though, it seemed like that was all I wanted since his injury, and now I almost felt like shouting, "His wheelchair is in the back. He's paraplegic!" Huh, I wonder where that came from.

We pulled into our usual bike shop. Dad passed up the handicapped spot and chose one at the edge of the lot that left room beside the truck for me to pull his wheelchair up to him. I used to bug him about that but he said he didn't have to be near to the store because he could roll up there just fine. What he really needed was the protected space beside the truck for the wheelchair. Whenever he could find that kind of spot in a regular space, he left the handicap spots open.

This was the shop where I had my close encounter with Strider. It still gives me the creeps, and I watch over my shoulder whenever I go back. I hadn't run into him since I saw him in his camp. I wonder if he would react to me any differently now. I'd just as soon not find out. Despite the association with Strider, the bike shop was a very cool place. Good music was always cranking. There were always half a dozen conversations going on about bikes and music and outdoor sports. People who came in there really enjoyed their bikes, so they were generally in a good mood and enjoyed talking with other people about their rides. It was a very friendly place and the guys at the shop knew Dad from all his bike projects. That didn't mean we got faster service. In fact, I'm sure it slowed things down. They yelled "hi" to him and asked him how he was doing while they continued to work with their other customers. Dad did the rounds and then cruised to the back of the counter where he knew they would have to go to get the cable. The shop was packed and it looked like we would be there a while. Dad was talking with a new guy who was working on a bike on a work stand. Soon it became apparent that the new guy was not having success with his project. He called to Mark, the owner, and asked for a hand. Mark said he would be a few minutes. The new guy flailed a bit longer and then just stopped.

"Is that an XRT?" It was my dad about to give advice. "They're supposed to come off without a crank puller but they don't always work. If the retaining ring spins, it won't push the crank out. Sometimes you have to hold it with something. Do you have a pin tool?"

"A what?" asked the new guy.

"Something to hold the ring. Could I give it a try?"

The new guy looked at Mark doubtfully. I was sure they had rules against customers working on other customers' bikes.

"Thanks Jeff," said Mark, and the new guy stepped back and Dad rolled up to the tools. He grabbed an odd looking thing and showed the new guy what wasn't supposed to turn on the crank. Soon, he and the new guy were up to their elbows in tools and parts, and it didn't look like Dad was going to back off until the bike was done. It also looked like he was having a great time. I watched for a while and then started exploring the shop. I figured I could kill a little time shopping for my fantasy bike.

As I rounded a corner, I just about ran into one of the climber guys from the Ravine.

"Katie Brown," he said.

"Hi Jake."

"Have you been getting out to the Ravine much?" he asked.

"Yeah, but I haven't seen you guys out there much lately."

"Nah, since it's cooled off some, we've been getting out to the park to do some real climbing. Do you get out there at all?"

"No, it's a little far to bike."

"Oh yeah," he said looking down at me and remembering that I was a little kid. How humiliating. "Well, you ought to ride out with us sometime."

I looked up at him in disbelief. He couldn't be serious. No way would those guys take a pre-teen girl with them. Beyond all sense, I was just starting to get excited about the idea when I saw the blank look on his face. This wasn't an actual invitation, he was just making conversation.

"That would be great," I said, trying not to show too much enthusiasm. "Say hi to the guys for me."

"Yeah, don't wire all the Ravine routes without us."

"Not to worry. See ya."

"Yeah, later."

I watched him walk up to the counter. Despite my best intentions, I drifted off into fantasy land picturing myself roped up and climbing sport routes out at the park. Now that would be a great way to spend a Saturday. I believed I could do it if I really got an invitation. I had been climbing there with my family since I could walk. I used to carry a little pack with my harness and water and my favorite stuffed animal. Now I could easily carry my own pack with everything I would need. And, obviously, I no longer needed Fluffy. The hike in and out would be no problem. I knew how to put on my harness and tie into the rope. I couldn't lead or belay the big guys, but I could help coil ropes and I wouldn't be any trouble. I thought about the bouldering routes in the Ravine. How hard did these guys climb? Would I be able to get off the ground on the routes they would choose at the park? I could do a lot of the routes in the Ravine that they did. I decided I needed to get them to talk about the routes they're climbing in the park so I'd have an idea if I could do any of them. The hardest climb I had done there was a 5.8, but that was almost two years ago and I'd been bouldering a lot since. I knew I had improved. I decided to ask Dad about some 5.9 and 5.10s that I should try.

The thought of Dad brought me back to reality. There I was, standing in the middle of the bike shop staring off into space. I was so out of it. I checked my chin for drool (it was clean) and looked for Dad. He was no longer working on the bike. I found him at Mark's office. They each had a beer and they were talking excitedly about setting a course for a mountain bike race. I watched them for a while without them noticing me. Dad looked so great. I hadn't seen him so alive since his injury. They pulled out a topographic map and Dad pointed out some obscure little canyon that he thought should be included in the route. Eventually, Mark seemed to assure Dad that they would try to include his recommendation and thanked him for helping out.

"I guess I better get moving on my girl's project," Dad said as he rolled out of the office towards me. "Thanks for letting me get my hands greasy."

"Think about that offer," said Mark. "I'm serious, I'd like to have you around."

We stopped at the counter and got the cable. I watched Dad put his wallet back into the pack on his wheelchair and noticed his cell phone in there. Finally, the pack was getting some good use. On the way home I asked Dad about Mark's comments.

"Hey Dad?"

"Yeah?"

"What was Mark talking about?"

"Oh, they're re-routing the Sage Hill Mt. Bike race this year, and I had some suggestions for a part of the route."

"After that."

"After the race?"

This was so typical of my dad. Unless I was absolutely specific about my question, he would keep avoiding it by acting ignorant.

Of course, that just proved to me that he and Mark were talking about something important.

"No, Dad. After you talked about the race, he said something about an offer."

"Oh, yeah. He offered me a job at the bike shop."

I waited to see what else he would say about it but of course he volunteered nothing.

"Well?"

"Well what?"

"What kind of job? Could you do it? Are you going to take it?"

"Well, I couldn't really do it now. I go to therapy three times a week, and I still have days when I can't leave the house because of bowel or bladder problems or leg spasms. Of course, he was actually talking about next spring when the bike business really takes off. Something might work out."

This was cool. Dad loved bikes. I knew he had been worrying about work. He had worked for the city at the water treatment plant. He and Mom say that the good insurance he had through the city really saved us because the drunk who hit him had no money or insurance. I thought Dad would go back to his old job a few weeks after the injury, but he said they could only take him back full-time, and he kept having problems that prevented that. I had started to think he would never work again but the bike shop sounded like a good possibility.

I looked over at him as we drove home. He looked like I did when I was dreaming about climbing at the park. He was obviously in Lala land. It's about time he had something to look forward to.

Back home, he put me to work on the bike. This was the part I was worried about. He could probably replace all the cables in a few minutes, but he was clearly going to have me do it. In the past, he stood over me watching me try to do what he described. With him watching me I could never do it right. This day was different though. He showed me how to get started with pulling cables and measuring the cable housing.

"Do you think you can work on this yourself for a bit?" he

asked.

"Sure," I said, probably sounding a little too eager to get him to give me some space.

"I think I'll try to set something up to let me access my tools."

I looked above his work bench where a lot of tools hung on pegboard. He couldn't reach a single thing over the bench.

"Eventually I should lower the whole bench and get rid of the stuff beneath it. But for now, I was thinking of something that would hang off the front and hold the bike stuff."

"That sounds great Dad. Let me know if I can help."

He started to work on a tool rack and left me to work on the cables by myself. I did much better without him hovering. I asked him questions about the cable cutter and he was helpful and then went back to his project. A couple of times he asked me to hold or reach something for him. This was actually a fun way to work together. I had to put up with his classic rock radio station, but other than that, it was nice. By the time I finished my cables, he had the basic form of a lowered tool rack in place. I think the idea of working at the bike shop had energized him. I could see that he would be modifying and perfecting his tool rack for a long time. He helped me adjust the brakes and shifters with the new cables and then rolled out into the driveway to watch me test ride it. We had to adjust one of the shifters a couple of times but got it working smoothly.

"You know, they make hand-bikes that I could ride," he said when I was putting up my bike. "We could ride together again if I get one of those."

"That would be so awesome Dad. Can you get one?"

"I'll look into it. I think they're kind of expensive, but I'd sure like to work something out."

I decided to go look them up on the internet. I think he only buys bikes at thrift shops and garage sales. I'm pretty sure he won't find a handbike there. He went back to work on his tool rack. I went inside, cleaned up and did an internet search. The handbikes looked really cool. They also had downhill bikes that he could ride and a system for cross country skiing. The more stuff I saw, the more I knew I was right, and Walter was wrong. Dad needed to be getting back out. Not watching sports on some stupid big screen but getting outside. There was a lot of stuff he could do again. Next time I talked with Walter I wouldn't back down so easily. I printed out some pages for Dad with info and phone numbers, and I bookmarked some of the best sites.

CHAPTER 8:
CLIMBER GUYS

The next week went by without any major events. I rode out to the Ravine Wednesday. None of the guys were there. I was really on. I sent every problem I had ever done before and got a new move on a nasty little problem called Piece Of Cake that was anything but. I blasted back on the trails and into town. Riding the streets in the evening I thought about riding with Dad. I'm not big on road riding, but on a warm summer evening, I think I could just ride around town all night. I like the way you silently coast by peoples' houses and yards and get a glimpse of what everyone is doing. The kids on swings, the barbecue grills smoking on back decks. As evening falls, the lights come on in the houses and you can see families moving around inside. I always imagine their conversations, their problems and excitements. I had never imagined anyone inside in a wheelchair.

As I got closer to home, I began to wonder what it looked like to a stranger riding past our house. I coasted by and looked. Dad's truck was sitting in the driveway. Mom wasn't home yet. Nothing about the truck or the outside of the house gave away Dad's injury. Some houses would need a wheelchair ramp, but ours is on one level. Dad can bump his wheelchair over the little threshold in the doorway. Inside, the kitchen lights were on, but I couldn't see anyone moving around. Duh, in a wheelchair, Dad couldn't be seen through the kitchen window. I had never noticed that. Mom and I could stand at the sink and watch the activity of the neighborhood. Dad could probably only see the sky through that window.

I turned around at the neighbor's house and rode back into our drive. Nobody was home but Dad. Walter was still at practice. Dad was in the kitchen. He was making pizza. I hung up my backpack and washed my hands to help him roll out the crust.

"How did you cut your hand?" he asked.

I saw that I had some scrapes on the back of my knuckles. "I was doing some bouldering." I was a little worried about telling him. He might not want me all the way out at the Ravine by myself. I watched closely and a bit nervously for his reply. He looked like he was starting to say something several times but stopped himself. Finally, he answered.

"A little climbing huh? Did you have fun?"

"Yeah, it was a low gravity day. I pulled some new moves."

"Cool. Here, help slice these peppers."

That was it. That was the entire conversation about climbing. The good news is he didn't find out where I climb and restrict it. The bad news is, this was just weird. Dad loves climbing. He talks about it with anyone. "Did you have fun?" was not talking about it. "What did you climb? What was the new move? How long did it take you?" That would be talking about it. I decided I couldn't let this go. I couldn't let Dad keep avoiding everything. Climbing, being outdoors, I had just seen the spark in his eyes in the bike shop. I couldn't let him shut down again.

"Oh man, pizza is perfect! I'm starved." It was Walter back from practice. "Dad, we must have run a million sprints today. I know that sounds like hyperbole but really, I counted to at least nine hundred thousand before my brain went numb."

"Hyperbole" was Walter's new word. He found a way to work it into conversation daily. Next time you think your brother is annoying remember Walter. Obviously, I was not going to have a meaningful conversation with Dad now. I just ignored their football babble and finished the pizzas.

Friday was another home football game. Walter said the coach had reviewed the special teams play from the first game and blamed two guys on the other side of the field for the mess-up in the first game. Those two had to run laps at every practice during the week, but the coach was putting them all back onto kickoff coverage again. Walter talked constantly about how he was supposed to cover one side of the field and how he planned to watch his side but to go wherever the ball carrier went. He was determined to get in on a tackle even if he was only in for one play again. Other than listening to him talk about his game plans, I didn't really get a chance to talk with him all week. It was amazing how little we saw of each other these days. I thought a lot about our talk after the first game and hoped we would have some time to hang out again.

After school Friday I went home with Sierra. Leah also came over. Sierra's mom was going to take us to the game together. We had her drop us off about an hour early. As she pulled her van away from the curb, we waved and watched her leave the parking lot. Then, instead of going into the stadium, we walked a couple blocks to the quickie mart. We had seen older kids hang out there before games last year and decided it was time for us to check it out. We saw no one in the parking lot and went in to get some gum. Just inside the door were three of the guys who climb at the Ravine. I wouldn't have thought much about it except that Leah practically squealed.

"That's Jake Denton! He's in my sister's class. Gawd, he's so cute!"

I wasn't going to have the climber guys see me giggling with a couple of schoolgirls. While Sierra and Leah whispered to each other, I headed to the back of the store. I stared at the display of sodas and tried to figure out how to get out of the store without embarrassing myself or insulting my girlfriends.

"Hey it's Katie Brown." The guys came around an end aisle and walked up to me.

"I hear you're coming out to the park with us one of these days?"

I looked around for Sierra and Leah. They must have stayed at the front of the store.

"Sure," I said. "Anytime."

"Dude! Chin up contest." Jason had jumped up and grabbed the pipe that held the sprinkler system.

"Dude! Mountain bike injury." Jake pointed to a large square of gauze on his elbow. The bandage was half-torn and dirty. Multiple layers of tape struggled to stick the gauze to his arm but were failing miserably. The wound extended beyond the edges of the haggard bandage where the blood was congealed with more dirt. Jason dropped from the pipe and suddenly Jake lifted me into the air by my waist. He must have held me straight over his head and I had to grab the pipe to keep from falling over.

"Katie Brown will take my turn."

"Come on," said Conner. "Girls can't do pull-ups."

"Katie Brown can. If she can't do a chin up, I'll buy."

"Three chin-ups," said Conner who was sounding less confident.

"Deal."

Everyone looked up at me. I was already getting tired just from hanging there but I was sure I could do three chin-ups.

"If I try, you've got to take me climbing."

"Only if you can do the three pull-ups."

I had thought I could do three, now I was sure of it. I cranked out three and then pulled one more with the adrenaline that came from the success. Jake grabbed my waist and lowered me down.

"You're buying," he said to Conner. "And I guess you're going climbing with us." This was followed by an awkward pause broken eventually by Sierra clearing her throat to get our attention. She and Leah were standing at the other end of the aisle.

"Great," I said. "I better get going. See ya." I tried to get away before my girlfriends joined in but halfway down the aisle Leah took a shot.

"Are you guys going to the game?"

The guys looked over like they had no awareness that Sierra and Leah were even in the store. Then grabbed their drinks and headed to the counter.

"What do you think Conner? Should we go cheer for the big football heroes?"

"Smells like school spirit to me."

"Maybe you could beat one of the big, fat lineman in a chin-up contest."

Their insults started to get more severe as I bolted out the door with Sierra and Leah in hot pursuit.

"You know those guys! How do you know those guys?"

"Forget that! How do they know you?" The inquisition began.

"I see them sometimes when I go bouldering. I don't really know them."

"I want to go bouldering."

"Yeah, you never take us with you."

"You don't climb."

"We didn't know Jake was there."

"Come on, let's go to the game."

"Do you think they're coming to the game?" Leah looked back towards the quickie mart.

"No, they are not coming to the game. I don't think they're football fans."

"Didn't they say something about school spirit?"

I think the girls kept gabbing and giggling all the way to the stadium. I went into one of the spacey trances they always kid me about. I was just realizing that Walter was in school with these guys. He probably saw them all the time. He could be hanging out with cool, climber guys instead of practicing football till dark every night. He must be more messed up than I had thought. I wondered if he would have been going to the park to climb after school if Dad hadn't been injured. Here we go again. How different things might have been. If Walter was climbing with these guys, I would definitely get to climb at the park with them. I wanted to feel mad because it would have felt so much better than the deep feelings of loss and hurt that were sapping all my energy. I couldn't even ball up my fist. I tried. Of course, that's when I realized that Leah and Sierra had stopped at the entrance to the stadium, and I was still walking. I tried to smile as I turned around.

"Where do you go when you do that?"

"It must be someplace far away. You're lucky you don't get hit by a car or walk off a cliff. How do you stay alive when you go climbing?"

That was an interesting observation. One of the things I like about climbing is that it forces me to attend. I can't drift off when I'm clinging to a tiny ledge. Instead, I'm totally focused on everything that I can see and feel. I love that sensation.

"Hellooooo?"

Oops, I had done it again. Instead of answering, I led the way into the stadium. The crowd in the stands gave the girls a thousand people to talk about so they seemed to forget about the climber guys. I looked around until I found Mom and Dad. They were sitting down on the field again. I had forgotten to ask Dad about that. Maybe after the game.

This time we received the kickoff. Walter blocked some guy, so I assume he did okay. I watched a bit of the game and talked with friends and drifted off occasionally to consider whether I might get to go climbing with the guys. I really paid attention to the game when we had a kickoff. Walter lined up on the near side, and I could practically see the energy radiating off him. The kick went straight down the field. Walter went straight down his side, about a third of the way. Then he saw that the guy returning the ball was heading straight up the middle. Walter faked to the outside and cut to the inside. The guy trying to slow him down got completely off balance. Walter shoved him hard and sprinted towards the ball carrier. I watched the guy fall backwards and roll. I wondered if that was legal. I was sure he wouldn't fall for it again. The whistle blew, and I looked to the center of the field where there was a large pile up. Walter climbed out from somewhere in the stack. Dang it. I didn't see what happened. It sure looked like he did something good. I tried to tell by watching how he ran off the field. No idea. He took his place on the sideline near the coach. Just like last game, he kept vibrating and following the coach around. At least this time it didn't look like the coach was going to smack him. The game continued pretty much like that. Walter got to play on every kick and punt. He seemed to be involved in several plays and our team won.

I spent the night at Sierra's. She and Leah got all freaky again about Jake at the quickie mart.

"Did you see how easily he lifted you? He's so strong."

"Oh man, if he put his hands around me like that...."

I had to start a pillow fight just to shut them up. We had a great time. It was almost 2:00 in the morning when Sierra's mom finally stopped yelling at us to go to sleep and fell asleep herself. We snuck down to the kitchen and got bowls of cereal and chocolate chips for a snack. The ringing phone woke us at 10:00 the next morning. It was a beautiful sunny morning. We laid in bed talking until Sierra's mom brought the phone up. It was Dad calling to find out when I was coming home. That was kind of weird. I couldn't figure out why they would care. We didn't have anything scheduled for the day. I agreed to come home in time for lunch, and we were so slow getting up that I barely made it.

I rode my bike into the garage and walked in through the kitchen door.

"Surprise!" Mom, Dad, and Walter stood under a huge birthday banner wearing party hats. This was a surprise. My birthday wasn't until next week. Dad rolled up and gave me a party hat.

"Happy Birthday, sweetie. I know you are planning to go skating with your friends to celebrate next weekend, but we wanted to have a family celebration. Hope you don't mind two parties."

Everybody hugged me, even Walter. Mom got all teary eyed. I swear, nobody ever cried in my house before Dad's injury. Now every little thing brings a flood of tears from somebody. I started to mist up a little bit too.

We had grilled cheese (my favorite) and ice cream with devil's food cake (also my favorite). Then they brought in presents. Walter gave me a CD. Mom got me a purse ("to put my female stuff in," she said). Then they all gathered around and handed me a small envelope. Clearly, this was the big gift and they all seemed so excited about it. I took the envelope and looked at Walter. He smiled knowingly. What the heck could they put in an envelope that would be so exciting? I tore it very slowly (mostly to irritate Walter who likes to rip into things). The certificate inside was from a local climbing guide service. A day of guided climbing at the park. This was way cool. I just started crying. They all looked alarmed, which made me cry more, and I got up and ran to my room. I know this sounds like a cliché, but I threw myself onto my bed and buried my head in the pillow. Mostly I think I was mad at myself for crying. Which, of course, made me cry more. I kept thinking that I should be happy, and I tried to make myself stop crying. No luck.

Eventually, Mom came in and sat beside me and stroked my hair. She didn't say a thing. I didn't look up, but I think she was crying a little too. Finally, I seemed to run out of tears. I pulled my head out of the pillow and Mom handed me a tissue.

"Great gift huh?" Mom smiled and dabbed her tears. I blew my nose and reached for another tissue.

"Sorry," I said. "I hope I didn't hurt anyone's feelings."

"No, Dad has stopped trying to figure out why women cry, and Walter hasn't started yet. They're probably just finishing off the cake and talking football."

"I do love the gift. And I hate it. I shouldn't have to go climbing with a guide, I should climb with Dad."

"I thought that's what this was about. There are a lot of things we would all like to do with Dad again. I don't know how to handle it. I try to be happy for all the things we did with him when he could walk. There were so many times when we could have stayed at home and watched TV or mowed the lawn and instead, we got out and played. I'm thankful for every one of those memories. I'm also happy that we still have Dad, and we can still be with him and do a lot together. There are things he won't do again. But you don't have to stop baby. You can still go climb and you can have a good time. Dad will love to hear about your adventures."

"But he doesn't. I told him I went climbing the other day, and he wouldn't even talk about it. I'm afraid it will just make him feel worse if I go climbing."

Mom gave me a hug. "He's still trying to figure it all out honey. I know he wants you to climb and have fun. Try it out. Go with the guide, have a great time and tell Dad all about it. He was really excited about getting this for you. I know he'll be into it."

CHAPTER 9: KYLE

The weekend finally came. Walter, the football team, and the cheerleaders left school early on Friday for an away game. Sierra, Leah, and Kate came home with me to celebrate my birthday. We were going skating after supper. Even though just the four of us were going for my birthday, I knew a lot of kids from my class were going that night. Mom served home-made mac and cheese at my request. And as a special treat for my birthday, Dad said he wouldn't complain about it (even though he says he hates it).

After supper my friends and I changed clothes and braided each other's hair to get ready to go skating. Dad looked in on us once and made fun of us for "getting all dolled up" to skate. He said we should be putting on knee pads instead of hair bows. I think he was picturing a skate-board park rather than a skating rink. We were just planning on gentle circles and good music and snacks, not jumps and 720s and flips.

Mom drove us to the rink. We were pretty pumped because we knew so many kids were going to be there. Kate kept talking about Kyle. He is the athlete in our class. He spends a lot of time at a skateboard park, plays on all the sports teams, and snowboards in the winter. I think every girl in my class has a crush on him. I hadn't thought much about him until our teacher put us on a project together a couple of weeks ago. Until then, I don't think he knew my name. There always seem to be two or three girls harassing him or messing with his stuff or doing other stupid things to get his attention. It seemed the only way to talk to him was to compete with that foolishness, so I had never talked to him. The day that Kyle and I got put on the same project, Alyssa actually shoved me in the lunch line. Like I did something wrong to get together with Kyle. Anyway, we were supposed to make a roller-coaster for a marble and identify a bunch of things for a science project. We were supposed to label things like the point of highest kinetic energy, the point of peak velocity and to calculate the average velocity. We turned out to be a great team. I'm always creating things and had a lot of ideas for designing the track. Kyle was actually interested in the calculations because he could relate them to skateboarding. We put a half-pipe in our coaster. Kyle had to make sure that the marble "caught some air" when it entered the half-pipe. I have to admit, it looked pretty cool. When the other girls weren't bugging Kyle, we had fun and the teacher was so impressed with Kyle's enthusiasm that I think we got a better score than we would have otherwise. However, we finished the project a week ago and hadn't spoken to each other since. Lately, Kate had been trying Alyssa's strategy of being so annoying that Kyle couldn't help but notice her.

Finally, we got to the rink. Mom gave me some extra money to buy treats for my friends since this was part of my birthday celebration. We all chose in-line skates and sat where we could check out the crowd while we changed. Most of the people we expected hadn't arrived yet, so we skated some warm-up laps. Kate could skate. She was amazingly good. She kept spinning around backwards and talking to us while we skated. Leah and I were just good enough to skate forward and not fall down unless someone cut us off or got in our way. We stayed close to the rail most of the time.

After a few laps we got drinks and hung out, talking about everybody as they arrived and started skating. Kyle showed up with Michael. Michael is my enemy. Everything he does annoys me. Most of the time, he doesn't even try. He recites a rap song nonstop. It is the most irritating song ever. He "accidentally" destroyed my science project last year when he drank one of the formulas (he had to go to the nurse's office). He said he thought it was the cup he had been drinking from. Michael and Kyle zoomed around twice as fast as anyone else, spinning backwards and doing tricks. But soon, there was such a flock of other kids hanging around with them that they could hardly move. We skated for hours. Most of the time I just went around with Leah. We both fell a couple of times. Once I biffed right in front of the seats and Kyle (who I honestly didn't know was there) stepped up to the floor to ask if I was alright. How embarrassing. Later, Kate joined in with Alyssa and some of the other Kyle fans trying to get his attention. I was just tasting my ice-cream when Leah pointed to the floor. Kate was dramatically losing her balance and starting to fall right in front of Kyle. We both laughed as he juked around her and kept going while she flailed to the floor. The night was so fun. They had black lights that made some clothes glow and smoke and a strobe light that made all the skaters look all jerky.

We ordered every kind of good food they had. Candy, nachos, popcorn and hotdogs. I had stopped eating red meat last year. Walter loved to make fun of me while he was snarfing steak. He would love to see me now, munching a hotdog that was probably made of cow lips, chicken butts and pig snout. But we were on a roll. It was a birthday party, and we were celebrating.

While we ate, we watched Kyle and Michael skate. A couple of other guys started a jumping contest. They would skate around the rink and then cut across to the exit that led to the men's room. The floor was carpeted there and sloped down. Just as they left the rink, they would jump as far as they could onto the carpet. They were moving so fast that they would slam in through the bathroom door. I had seen this when I was here last time and the people working here stopped it as soon as they saw it. The guys knew that too, so they knew they would probably get only one jump before they got yelled at. Kyle was the last one up. We watched him circle to pick up speed and then rocket toward takeoff. Just before he got to the edge of the rink, a little boy cut right in front of him. Kyle tried to squeeze between the little boy and the rail and almost made it. Only his right leg hit the rail and sent him spinning down the carpet. He smashed head first, going backward into the bathroom door. The door flew open, then swung back and smacked him again in the back of the head. It looked awful. He just crumpled to the floor. I was sure he was dead. Leah jumped up and ran towards him. I just watched. I honestly didn't think he'd get up.

The manager ran over. He could see from where Kyle was laying that he had been trying to do the jump. I guess I know why they try to stop it. Kyle saw the manager and hopped up. Unbelievable.

"Whoa," he said. "He started looking at the floor. "I just tripped on something by the door. Really..." he looked up at the manager, "somebody could get hurt on the garbage on this floor." He leaned forward to pick up a cup off the floor and winced and turned kind of white. Michael grabbed him and helped him to a chair at the table beside mine. The manager just scowled at him and picked up a couple pieces of trash. He muttered something about stupid kids as he walked off. Leah now came back to my table. She hadn't even gotten to Kyle before he got up.

"Dude, man. I thought you were dead. That looked heinous," said Michael. "Does it hurt?"

"Hell yes it hurts. Dang, I got a huge lump on my head," Kyle rubbed the back of his head. "My leg is totally screwed," he said as he slowly straightened his right leg. He was still kind of pale looking.

"Well? You going to skate more?" Michael didn't seem to recognize that Kyle was injured.

"Go ahead. I'm gonna sit here for a while."

Michael skated off and soon the crowd that had gathered dispersed. Leah, who had wanted to do something to help since Kyle fell, finally found her voice.

"Would you want to put some ice on that knee?"

Kyle looked at her and looked at his leg. "That would probably be good."

Leah hopped up and launched an ice search. Suddenly I found myself alone with Kyle as he rubbed his leg.

"Pretty stupid huh?"

"Does it hurt a lot?"

"Mostly my knee. Man, I hope I didn't screw it up."

"What are you going to do?"

Kyle kind of smiled and looked at the half a hot dog I was still holding in my hand. "I'm going to put ice on my leg and try to talk someone into getting me some food.

Now I looked at the hot dog and quickly set it down. "Do you want me to get you a hot dog?"

"No, but I'd really like some nachos and a coke." I started to get up.

"No, wait," he continued. I stopped. "Wait till your friend gets back with the ice." I sat down. Now what? This was kind of nice. He wanted me to stay. He didn't know Leah's name.

"Oooh," he moaned while trying to get his billfold out of his back pocket.

"Don't. I'll get it." I held up a wad of bills. "Birthday money."

"Cool. Is it your birthday?"

I looked at the money and looked back at him and we laughed. Leah walked up with small bag of ice, and I took off for the nachos.

I walked back toward the table with the nachos. Kyle had his leg up on a chair with the ice on his knee. He was watching the skaters. Beside him, Leah was talking and laughing. As I approached, I could see her lips moving but couldn't hear her over the music and noise. Kyle didn't appear to hear her or even to be aware that she was talking. He was just staring out at the rink.

"....he looked so mad stomping off with that paper cup. It was sooo funny," Leah was recounting Kyle's injury for him.

When he saw me, Kyle pulled a chair in between his and Leah. I don't know if he wanted me close or if he just wanted a break from Leah. I plopped the nachos onto the table and grabbed one as I sat down. I handed the coke to Kyle. He took a long drag of the coke and his color seemed to come back almost instantly. It was like medicine.

"Thanks."

"Sure."

We ate nachos and watched the skaters. Leah tried to start conversations three or four times before giving up and joining the skaters. Michael tried to provide entertainment. He skated by backwards. He skated by squatting really low beside a row of little kids. He skated by beside a very fat woman with his arm behind her back as if he had his arm around her. I was kind of hoping she would notice and deck him. A smack with one of those massive arms and he would have been in worse shape than Kyle.

"What do you think is the kinetic energy potential of that woman just before she falls on Michael?" Kyle asked.

"I don't know, but I'd love to see it." We laughed at the image.

"Come skate with me," said Leah as she zipped up beside us. "We'll have to leave in a couple of minutes."

I looked over at Kyle. He said nothing but just watched me. "I think I'm done for tonight," I said.

"Oh, come on, just a couple more laps," she pleaded. Kyle kind of smiled.

"Alright, just a couple." I rolled my eyes towards Kyle as Leah pulled me out of my seat.

We zoomed around the rink fast and then cruised a couple of slow laps. I could tell that Leah wanted to talk about Kyle, but the music was too loud to talk without yelling. I'm sure she wanted this conversation to be a bit more private. Suddenly the lights began to flash, and smoke rolled out of the walls. They announced the last song and seemed to crank the volume even louder. I lost all track of Kyle while we spun around in a blur of light and dark and smoke. When the song ended and the lights came up, I didn't even know what part of the rink we were on. A quick scan revealed Kyle across the rink talking to someone who seemed to be squatting down in the aisle. No, he was in a chair. Oh Gawd, a wheelchair. How did Dad always manage to nose into my stuff?

I returned my skates and put on my shoes before going over to Dad. I was hoping they would finish talking and split up. No such luck.

"No," Dad was saying, "The ACL is the anterior cruciate ligament. That's the one on the front side of your leg. I tore that one in college. This is the scar from that surgery.

One thing he hadn't changed since his injury was his habit of wearing shorts. In all kinds of weather, you could count on Dad to be out in shorts. It seemed that most people in wheelchairs wear long pants, like they want to cover up, or protect their legs that have no feeling. Not Dad. He hangs those dead legs right out in front of him for everyone to see. I watched for Kyle to cringe as Dad traced the scar on his leg. Kyle was unfazed.

"Good, maybe this is just a bad bruise. I can move it okay, it just hurts. It looks like your daughter is ready to go." Kyle spotted me.

"Hey babe," said Dad looking me over from head to toe. "No big bruises on you?"

"No, but then again, I didn't try any record setting jumps through closed doors."

Kyle smiled, "I must have really thumped my head. All I remember is tripping over a piece of trash. I think it's against the rules to jump in here."

"Trash can be tricky," Dad played along. "Let's hit the road kid. Who am I chauffeuring home tonight?"

I said goodbye to Kyle and gathered up the girls. We said goodbye to Leah and Kate, who were leaving with Kate's mom. They gave me big, happy-birthday hugs. With Dad in the car, Sierra and I didn't talk about anything but the skating and the food. We dropped her off and drove home listening to the radio. I was tired when I got home, but since Walter wasn't back yet, I tried to stay up for a while. I flipped through the TV channels on Dad's big TV. I think I'd only checked it out once before. With all my complaining about it, I really couldn't spend much time watching it. Luckily, there never seemed to be anything on that

I'd want to watch. It took me almost an hour to go up through all the channels and back down again. About then, Walter came home. He looked beat, but content and headed straight to bed. I turned out the lights and locked the doors and went to my room.

CHAPTER 10:
HOME SICK

I guess I should have gone to bed right when I got home, when I was feeling tired. When I finally did try to go to sleep, I found that I was wired. I kept thinking about Kyle and Leah, and Kate's skating, and that stupid hot dog. My stomach was in knots like I was nervous about something. I felt really hot even though it was a pretty cool night. I kept pulling my sheet on and then kicking it off. Sometimes I felt hungry but sometimes my stomach was a little upset. I turned on my light and pulled out my diary, but I really didn't have enough energy to write anything. The latest entry was three weeks old. My plans to write in it every day always fell through. Once again, I closed it without adding anything and turned out the light. I flopped around in bed for a long time. Eventually, I must have fallen asleep because I woke up with a start. Something was wrong. My face was all sweaty but cold. I looked around the room. Everything looked okay, but something was wrong. Oh man, my stomach was on fire. Oook, I felt bad. All I could think of was that stupid hot dog. I could taste it, I could smell it. Everything I looked at reminded me of that dog. Oh man, I hate to throw up, but it sure felt like it was coming. I staggered down the hall to Mom and Dad's room. I leaned on Dad's shoulder.

"Dad, DAD. I'm sick Dad. I think I'm going to throw up."

"Go to the bathroom babe, I'll...."

I didn't wait for the rest of his sentence. I rushed to the bathroom. I plopped down on the floor and lifted the toilet seat. As bad as I felt, I still was able to pull down some toilet paper and wipe off the rim of the toilet. Sharing a bathroom with a brother really sucks. Oh man I hate to throw up. I rolled around on the floor holding my stomach feeling worse and worse. The sick feeling moved from my stomach through my whole body. As it approached my head, I thought I would die. Waves of sickness crashed through my skull, and I leaned over and puked. Then, all of the misery centered in my stomach. I heaved and heaved until everything was out, and then I heaved a couple more times. I was afraid I wouldn't be able to stop. The spasms in my stomach were totally out of my control. Oh man it stunk. I flushed the toilet and slumped back onto the floor. I spit a few times to try to get rid of the taste. Ooh, I had to get the taste out of my mouth. I was trying to get up to the sink when Mom came in.

"Here you go sweetie." She wetted a washcloth for my face and filled a drinking glass with water. "Just swish a little in your mouth and spit it out. Try not to swallow any."

While I was rinsing my mouth, she got a scrunchy to hold my hair back. She rinsed the wash cloth and wiped my face again. She really was good at this. It may be strange, but in my family, it has always been Dad who gets up with us when we're sick. I wasn't even thinking about it when I ran into his room. I guess it's a lot harder for him to get up and moving now. He certainly couldn't sit on the floor beside me like Mom was doing.

"Thanks Mom. I think I'll be alright now." I still didn't feel good, but I was so much better than before I puked that I almost thought I felt good. Mom tucked me back in bed. I heard her wash her hands and walk back to bed. She hadn't gotten up at night for a long time. We learned very young not to try to wake Mom. She slept deeply, and it was hard to wake her up. Once when I was really little, I woke up scared in the middle of the night. I walked down the hall to Mom and Dad's room and went to her side of the bed and shook her arm to wake her. I tried about three times. Then, while I was standing there, she opened her eyes and saw me. She screamed. Later, she said she hadn't felt me shaking her and just woke up to somebody staring into her face. Anyway, her scream scared me half to death, so I screamed. Dad woke up to the two of us screaming at each other and it took about an hour for everyone to calm down and get back to sleep. So, I started waking Dad if I needed something. Since his injury, that didn't seem like such a good idea either.

I drifted back to sleep only to wake up in about an hour feeling all pukey and sweaty. I crawled out of bed and started down the hall. I didn't know who to wake. I turned back to the bathroom. Again, I laid on the floor until the sickness felt so bad I couldn't help but throw up. This time I didn't feel so much better afterward. I lay back on the floor. I tried to curl up on the small rug. The tile floor around it was cold. I pressed my forehead to the tile floor and felt better for a couple of minutes. There I could get a little whiff of the floor cleaner and escape from the puke fumes. I listened for Mom or Dad to come down the hallway, but no one stirred. Then my stomach cramped and I had to sit on the toilet. Diarrhea. And, I thought I might throw up again. I leaned forward and pulled the wastebasket out from under the sink. Oh crap I felt bad. I heard Walter close his bedroom door and realized I was moaning out loud. Finally, the stomach cramps let up. I tried to hold my breath and flush the toilet. I thought the smell was going to make me puke again. I literally crawled back to my bed. All by myself. I had never been sick without my mom or dad around. I felt kind of proud of myself. But also kind of lonely. Like I had lost something. And then I was asleep and probably slept for a while before I had another round of puking and pooping.

The next time I woke up it was light out. I heard Mom and Walter in the kitchen. I stayed in bed for a while then put on clean pajamas and went to the bathroom to brush my teeth. I couldn't get out of there fast enough. Just being there almost made me sick again. I staggered out to the living room and collapsed onto the couch.

"Our poor sweetie was sick last night," said Mom.

"No kidding, she rattled the windows with all that puking and belching," Walter, of course.

I moaned and held my stomach.

"Are you better today honey? I'm surprised you only threw up once."

"I was up two more times. I still feel pretty weak."

"You didn't get me? Oh baby, I'm sorry. You went through that all by yourself?"

"There really wasn't much you could do Mom. But thanks for getting up the first time."

"My goodness, you are growing up. When you're ready I'll get you some soda and toast."

"Ohhhh, not now." I laid back and closed my eyes. Mom and Walter went back to talking; football of course.

"I'm so sorry we couldn't come to your game," said Mom. "It was so far away. Next week you're back in town. We'll be there again. So, you did well?"

"Yeah, I made one tackle myself and got in on a couple of others. On the way back, coach Michaels said he might start putting me in at d-back on long yardage situations."

Mom looked at him. "You know I have no idea what that means."

"It means I might get to play more."

"Excellent."

I staggered out to the family room. Dad was on the couch, watching football. He actually stays in his wheelchair most of the day. He says the $350 cushion on the wheelchair is comfortable and protects his skin. Apparently, all that fidgeting that we kids do when we're supposed to sit still is actually good for us. Dad says that people with paraplegia often get skin sores because they sit on one spot too long. They don't feel anything, so they don't fidget and the blood supply to the skin gets cut off. He said that half of people with spinal cord injuries end up back in the hospital with bad skin sores and he's determined to be in the other half. When he first came home from rehab, he had a watch that beeped every twenty minutes to remind him to lift the pressure off his buns. Now, he does wheelies a lot in his chair to shift his weight. The one place he sits in the house is on this couch by the TV. He can transfer from the wheelchair onto the couch by sort of sliding himself over. Then, he uses his arms to move his legs into a fairly normal position. Sometimes he pulls them up onto the couch, and he looks really normal lying there. He says that legs are way heavier than we would expect, and it's a lot of work to pull them up. This time he was sitting up on the couch with his feet on the floor. I stood at the doorway and watched him. When he looked up at me, he smiled.

"Boomer Sooner, Boomer Sooner....." he started to sing softly. That's not how he usually sings it. He usually belts it out so that all the neighbors hear. I guess he was showing a little respect for my state of illness. The Oklahoma Sooners. What's up with that. We live in Oregon. Dad didn't watch much football before his injury, but he was always a Sooner fan. Every fall we have to hear about the new running back or linebacker. Every spring he tells us how highly the linebackers got drafted by the NFL. His definition of tough was to be the middle linebacker for the Oklahoma Sooners. Whenever he wanted us to do something difficult or when we complained about something being hard, he would say, "You're never going to make middle linebacker for the Oklahoma Sooners if you don't get tougher than that." By the time I was 4, I gave up explaining that I was a girl and was unlikely to play any position on any football team. Whenever he was impressed with something we did he would say, "I hope the Sooner's scouts saw that. Keep that up and you might have a shot at linebacker." The ultimate tough story was, of course, a climber. I read the book "Touching the Void" about a climber who fell on some remote peak in South America and broke his leg. His partner was trying to lower him down the mountain but accidentally lowered him over the edge of a cliff during the night. To keep from being pulled off with him, the partner cut the rope and the climber plunged over the cliff and into a crevasse. Left for dead, he spent the next few days crawling out of the crevasse, across a glacier, and down the mountain. He has to be the toughest man alive. I was talking to Dad about it after I read the book and he agreed.

Dad gave his ultimate toughness compliment, "That's a tough man. I know he's a climber and wouldn't do team sports. And, he's a Brit and thinks football is soccer. But I'm telling you. That guy is probably tough enough to play middle linebacker for the Oklahoma Sooners."

I slumped across the room and lay down on the couch with my head on his lap. How strange that he couldn't feel my head on his legs. I just wanted to snuggle up so tight to his legs that he would have to feel me.

"Sorry you were sick last night, babe. Wish I could have helped."

"There wasn't much anyone could do. Unfortunately, nobody could puke for me. It would have been nice if you had eaten that hot dog for me at the skating rink."

"Now you're asking for a bit much," he sounded like he was smiling, but I didn't look up. I was just feeling so much loss and sadness. He couldn't feel me on his lap, he couldn't get up to help me when I was sick. I tried to focus on the game. Alabama scored a touchdown. So, the game sucked too. I was wallowing in sadness when a drop of water landed on the side of my face. I looked up. Dad was watching the game, but I could see where tears had run down his face.

"Hey," I said. "They're only down by seven. They'll come back." I turned back to the TV before he could see my tears.

I drifted in and out of sleep during the game. At some point, Dad left, and I spent the day on the couch and ate a little soup for supper. I wasn't feeling too bad by bedtime. Man, I was glad it didn't happen next week when I had my climbing day. The next few days I tried to eat well and take vitamins to help me recover. I wanted to be in good shape for the climbing guide. None of my friends got sick, so it must not have been the hot dogs. But I won't be eating another one soon.

CHAPTER 11:
MORE KYLE

I didn't even try to go bouldering until Thursday. I felt pretty good by Tuesday but didn't want to push it. When I got to the Ravine, I kept thinking about the guided climbing day next Saturday. I wanted to get in a workout so I would be in shape, but I was also worried about getting hurt. Rock climbing can obviously be dangerous. Most injuries are strain injuries to fingers and hands and I know a couple of people who have broken ankles when they took long roped falls. That's about the worst that can happen unless you make a mistake. And even a little mistake can kill you when you're rock climbing. Bouldering is safer in a way. You are very unlikely to die. However, the risk of the little injuries, broken ankles and such, is much higher. Since you're not roped, you always fall on the ground. If you climb high or fall awkwardly, things break. My main concern on Thursday was to stay healthy for Saturday. Of course, that's when you are at the most risk; when you're really trying not to get hurt.

Instead of climbing the hardest problems, the ones that might strain my fingers, I decided to do laps on some easier problems. Not much risk because I'd done them a million times, but I could still get a good workout on them. I started up *Bunny Hop*, a simple little problem that starts with a leap (for us shorter types) up to a nice handhold. From there, it's a little like climbing a ladder from the underside. It's a little bit overhanging but the handholds are really good. No way of falling. So, I hopped up and grabbed the ledge. I smoothly worked through the moves. My feet and hands automatically found the little nubs and ledges. Bunny hop does go sort of high, but then you can traverse to the edge of the cliff and walk off.

I was just about to the top, with one last right hand hold before the traverse left. My feet were on solid, but tiny, ledges and I had a three-finger side pull for my left hand. I gradually leaned to the right to get the most out of the left side-pull. I slowly moved my right hand up and into the crack. The next moment was totally disorienting. I heard a rapid clicking sound and felt it vibrate on my right fingers. It's difficult to say a clicking sound can be angry, but it was clear that the thing making that noise was highly agitated. Something brushed my right fingers and my hand flew out of the crack. It didn't consult with my brain to see if it could let go. It just jumped backwards. The force of my right hand moving out threw my right foot back a fraction of an inch, just enough to take it off the ledge. With nothing holding up the right half of my body, I peeled off the wall. I pushed myself backwards so I could look down. I was plummeting towards a flat piece of land with only one rock about the side of a fractured bowling ball. As long as I missed that rock I would be okay. I positioned my feet to the sides of the rock and watched as it zoomed towards me. I was concentrating so much on my position that I didn't really prepare for the impact. My feet hit flat but my legs were not ready to catch me. After my feet hit, I continued slamming toward the earth. I put my hands out and went down into a forced hard squat. Even my head was thrown down and I felt crushed in a most awkward and scrunched up ball. At the last instant I feared that my face would be pummeled into the rock. There seemed to be nothing I could do to break the fall. I came to a stop with my nose against the rock. Not gently.

I rolled backwards and tried to stretch out. My back, legs

and neck had never bent so far. And my nose was starting to swell and run. I went through a gradual inventory. Feet moved, ankles, knees, hips. Eventually, I got my back straightened and rolled my head around on my neck. Everything worked. I just didn't want to look in a mirror. My nose felt huge. I dabbed it with the bottom of my t-shirt and walked back up to the rock. Glad nobody was watching that. I looked back up at the crack. A freakin' bat. I knew they sometimes lived in cracks in the rock and Dad had told me how they make a clicking noise when you disturb them. Eeew. I shivered with disgust and wiped my hand on my pants. I dabbed my nose on my shirt again. Eventually, I made a few moves on a traverse close to the ground but my heart really wasn't in it. Soon, I packed up my stuff and biked home; my bulbous nose dripping all the way. It might be ugly, but it wasn't going to stop me from climbing on Saturday, so I guess I was alright.

Although my nose felt swollen, it didn't really look different in the mirror. The next day I could see it was a little bluish, but fortunately, nobody at school noticed. The week couldn't go quickly enough for me.

Friday night I went to Walter's game. I tried to pay attention. I knew it was really important to Walter. Once I noticed that he was in the game when it wasn't a kick. I guess that means that he really was getting to play more. Okay, actually, I didn't see him in the game. I saw him coming off the field, so he must have been in. In the stands, I noticed that Kyle was limping still when he walked down the bleacher steps. It was a lot cooler than the previous game and Dad had a blanket around him. I stared at him for a long time. It was hard to believe that that was my dad; sitting in a wheelchair, huddled up in a blanket. This was the guy that ran behind me when I was learning to ride a bike. I never wanted him to let go of that seat. The first time he let me go on my own I heard him cheering me on. I looked back to see where he was and biffed hard. After that, he had to run beside me for miles until I got my confidence back. I watched him take a warm thermos from Mom. This is the guy who took me on my first backpacking trip and carried most of my stuff. He let me carry his sleeping bag, because it was lighter than mine, and he made me carry a bottle of water, because he's always had some stupid rule about carrying your own water. I remember feeling the straps dig into my shoulders after a couple of miles and then looking at the monster pack he carried with all our stuff. Walter and I used to wrestle him. Even right before his injury he would still pin us both at once. He seemed indestructible. He couldn't possibly be stuck in that chair.

"....I don't know where she goes. One minute she's here with us and the next......it's just like a shell of a body sitting in her seat. HELLO?" Sierra of course. Apparently, they had been talking about Kyle's fall last weekend and wanted me to say something.

"I'm going to go get a drink," I said and quickly started thumping down the bleacher steps. I was in no shape for a chat about Kyle's bruised knee.

Well, not with them anyway. Kyle was standing at the concession stand.

"How's your leg?" was the first thing out of my mouth.

"It's better. I guess that looked pretty stupid?"

"What?" I asked, worried that he had seen me spacing out in the stands.

"Me skating into the rail."

"Well, you looked like you were gonna make a long jump. And it looked better than flattening the little kid that zipped in front of you."

"Yeah, I guess that could have been ugly. Walter's having a good game."

"You know my brother?"

"You told me about him when we built our roller coaster. Not many sophomores get beyond special teams."

This would have been a good time to say something, but I was just staring at Kyle wondering why he was talking to me. He smiled and took his drink from the guy at the counter.

"What do you want?" he asked. "I think I owe you a coke and some nachos."

"Just a coke. Thanks. No, I mean, you don't owe me anything but I'm getting a coke."

"I got it," he said, paying the guy. We stepped away from the concession stand.

"Are you sitting with the pep club?" he asked, motioning to my friends who were all standing and cheering at something happening on the field.

"Yeah. Where are you sitting?"

"Oh, I've just been kind of wandering from place to place. Did you see the addition they're building on the stands for your dad?"

I must have looked like a dork at this point. I had no idea what he was talking about. They were building a new stadium on the edge of town but that didn't have anything to do with my dad.

"No?" I muttered.

"Come here. I'll show you."

We walked towards one end of the stadium where there were a pile of boards on the ground and some yellow tape marking off the area around it.

"They're putting a wheelchair platform up here so he can stay up at the level of the stands. I guess Mr. Jenkin's kid will sit there too. They should have a much better view from up here."

"Yeah." I wanted to tell him how different my dad was than Mr. Jenkins kid. Dad was normal. Ty Ty was "handicapped". I didn't want Kyle to lump them together.

"Are you sure your leg is okay?" I asked. It was supposed to be a subtle change of conversation, but since we had already talked about his leg, it was just an awkward, irrelevant comment.

"I won't be needing the wheelchair seating if that's what you're worried about." Kyle was smiling. A very nice smile.

"That's not what I meant. Thanks for the coke." I tried a new tack.

"Glad to."

Just to our right a cell phone rang with the scooby doo theme. We both looked over to see a way-too-skinny blonde answer her phone.

"I'm here where are you!" she positively squealed.

From our other side came an echoing squeal and we turned to see a more normal weight, bleached blonde yelling into her phone.

"I'm at gate C! Where are you?"

We turned back to skinny blonde. "NO! I'm at gate C. I'm right in front of the gate. You are not here!"

"It says gate C," said bleached blonde. "I really think I'm here. Where are you?"

This looked like it could go on all night. Kyle tried to intervene.

"Hey Daphne!" He yelled at skinny blonde. "She's over there!" Skinny blonde shook her head and pointed to the phone. Kyle turned to bleach head. "Yo, Thelma!" He pointed at her friend.

"I'm sorry, I couldn't hear you. Some guy is yelling at me." Thelma yelled in her phone.

"Me too!" answered Daphne.

Kyle took my hand (which felt really nice) and pulled me down into a squat so the blondes could see over us. After an ear-splitting squeal, bleach head ran past and hugged her partner.

"Nice work Shaggy."

"Shaggy? I've always thought of myself as more of a Scooby."

"Maybe," I smiled. He stood up and helped me up by the hand. He held it for just a little while after we stood up. We watched the blondes walking away. One continued to talk into her phone until the other reached up and closed it. "I think they make a better Paris and Nicole," I suggested.

"That they do," said Michael.

"That boy called me Daphne!" said skinny as the girls waved and headed down the stairs.

"Did you see those babes checking me out?" Michael arrived on the scene. "They want me bad."

"Yeah, Michael. I think you should go talk to them," Kyle

called his bluff.

"Naw, they'll just have to wait. I'm gonna watch some football."

I was sort of relieved that Michael came busting into the scene because I had no idea what to say or do next. On the other hand, it was really obvious that any conversation with Kyle was now over, and I was really bummed about that.

"I guess I'll get back to the pep club. See you later."

"Yeah," said Kyle.

"Let's roll," said Michael. And they were off.

I climbed back up the bleachers thinking about Kyle's comment about not needing a wheelchair. I was wondering if there was some insult of my dad in that comment. Back at my seat, my friends were all talking and paying no attention to the game. I looked out on the field and saw the trainers working on an injured player. I looked back at my friends. They were oblivious. I looked back to the field. It was one of our guys who was injured. It could be Walter. Just the thought of Walter injured like Dad was too much to take. I felt my legs buckle and I sat down on the step.

"What's the matter?" asked Leah.

"Who is it? Who is the injured guy?"

"Jack Garcia."

"JACK HAMMER!" yelled one of the other girls. He was just being helped to his feet. The crowd applauded politely. I scanned the bench and found Walter with a couple of other players listening to a coach. One of the other players sprinted onto the field to take Jack's place and the coach slapped him on the butt as he ran past. I don't know a lot about our football team, but everybody knows that Jack is a major defensive player. His name is called on a lot of tackles. I watched the trainers help him off the field. He wasn't putting any weight on his right side, and he looked like he was really hurting. I can't say I paid much attention to the rest of the game. Walter seemed to play a little more than before. I don't know if it was because of Jack's injury or because he was doing well.

I rode home with Mom and Dad. I would have liked to stay up to talk with Walter when he got home, but I was worried about getting good sleep before my climbing day. I checked my pack in the garage before I went to bed. All I needed to add was a cold water bottle in the morning. Right after breakfast the guide was going to pick me up and take me to the park. Despite my best efforts, I was still awake to hear Walter come home. I listened to him scrounging around in the kitchen for a while. I decided to go see him but was too comfortable to get up right then. I must have fallen asleep for a while because the next time I thought about getting up the house was dark and quiet. I spent the whole night waking and sleeping in short bursts.

CHAPTER 12:
GUIDED CLIMBING

I was so glad when it was finally light out. I think I was the first one up. I got my pack from the garage, rechecked it and added a full water bottle. I wanted to eat a healthy breakfast but was too excited to be hungry. Finally, I got myself to eat a bowl of cereal. I had a couple of energy bars in my pack, and I added an apple. I paced the kitchen and kept looking out at the driveway. A climbing guide named Jared was going to pick me up at 8:00. I still had half an hour to kill. I heard Mom and Dad waking up. I kept expecting Dad to come rolling into the kitchen to talk about my climb. I went into the family room and got the guidebook to the park. Sitting at the kitchen bar, I studied the possible climbs. I had no idea what level I would be able to climb. I hadn't been out to the park since before Dad's injury. It had probably been two years. I was like, 10. I know I had done some 5.8s.

If you don't climb, you probably don't know the rating system. It doesn't make much sense because it evolved over time. The way my dad explains it is that a long time ago, a bunch of climbers in Yosemite, California got together and picked 10 class 5 climbs from the easiest to the hardest they had done. Class 5 means you need to use gear. I guess class 4 would be a steep hike. Anyway, they numbered the 10 climbs from 5.0 – for the easiest, to 5.9 - for the hardest. That probably worked for a couple of weeks, but then someone climbed a harder climb and they numbered it 5.10, which really makes no sense because that's mathematically the same as 5.1. Anyway, they called it five-ten and that's where it stayed for a while. All the climbs that were harder than 5.9 were rated 5.10. As people got better at climbing, some of those climbs became a whole lot harder than others. They didn't want to go to 5.11 so eventually, they broke down the 5.10 climbs to 5.10a, b, c and d. When it became apparent that harder climbs could be done, they went to 5.11a then b, c and d, then 5.12 etc. My dad remembers when the first 5.13 was a big deal. Now there are 5.15s. Really sick overhanging stuff.

So, I climbed 5.8 a couple years ago, and I've been bouldering a lot and I'm a lot stronger than I was then. I'm sure I'll get a 5.9 but 5.10 is kind of the barrier between being someone who has climbed and being a climber. I want to be a climber, but it's hard for me to imagine climbing 5.10. I was paging through the guidebook looking at 5.9 and 5.10a routes when Mom came out. I was hoping it was Dad and I must have looked disappointed when I saw her. Nothing wrong with Mom, I just wanted to talk climbing with Dad.

"Sorry honey. Dad wanted to come check your pack and give you advice but he's having trouble with his bowel program. It doesn't look like he'll get out here before you leave."

"That's okay. I think I've got everything ready." Stupid bowel program. Trouble with his bowel program meant that he either couldn't go or that he went when he wasn't supposed to. Either way, he wasn't going to be out for a while.

"He said to make sure you have your harness and shoes," Mom smiled. "And I want to be sure you have food and water and sunscreen and bug repellent and a hat and a jacket and...."

"Mom, I'm good."

"Did you get some breakfast?"

"Yup."

"What time do you think you'll be home?"

"I have no idea. I'll climb as long as he keeps guiding."

"Well, be careful honey. I'm going to check on Dad. I'll be right back out."

Just as she left, an old pickup pulled into the drive. I grabbed my pack and yelled goodbye. I heard Mom and Dad both yell back as I headed out the door.

Jared grabbed my pack. He opened the cap on the back of the truck.

"Do you need anything with you for the ride?" he asked.

"I'm good."

He dropped my pack into the back and walked around to the driver's side. I climbed up into the passenger seat.

I glanced back at Dad's bedroom window as we pulled away. A wave of regret washed over me, and I felt like jumping out of the truck. I shouldn't be going with a guide. My dad's a climber. That's who I want to climb with. I stared out the window at the neighbors' houses. I seemed to be thinking about other peoples' lives a lot more lately. The truck accelerated as we pulled onto the highway. Once again, I realized I had been lost in my thoughts for a long time. I hope Jared hadn't asked me any questions while I was spacing out. I'm sure he wasn't thrilled to have to guide a kid. A psycho kid might be a little too much for him.

Now that I was mentally back in the truck with Jared, it seemed really awkward that we weren't talking. On the other hand, I was kind of relieved because I doubted that there was much we could talk about. We rolled on down the highway. Eventually I picked up the guidebook that was lying beside me on the seat.

"So, what do you want to do?" asked Jared.

"Climb," I said smiling. Jared didn't smile. He showed no expression as he continued to stare straight out the windshield. Oh crap, I thought. This is going to be a long day.

"How's your dad?" he asked.

Where did this come from? Was he punishing me for my stupid climb comment? I hate this. It seems that every adult has to ask about Dad every time they see me.

"He's good."

"Did you used to climb with him?"

"Yeah."

"What kind of stuff have you done?"

"Well, obviously, we haven't climbed out here for almost two years. Back then I did some of the 5.8s on top-rope. *Lite Dance, Kitty Face, Simple Slab*. Wow, those really sound wimpy don't they?"

"Yeah, maybe we should climb something like *Heinous Vomit Slinger* and round out your resume. Have you ever done any leading?"

"No."

"Do you want to?"

"Some day, but not today. I haven't been off the ground for a couple of years, but I have been doing quite a bit of bouldering. I'd like to just get up on some new climbs and see if I can send some harder routes."

Jared smiled. I was afraid I was using too much climber talk, trying to sound like a real climber instead of a 5.8 wannabe. Lead climbing is the person who goes up first. At a place like the park, the routes have bolts drilled into the rock. The first climber ties to the end of the rope and then links the rope through carabiners at each bolt. The partner on the ground plays out rope through a belay device. If the lead climber falls, the belayer stops the rope in her belay device and the rope jerks tight through the last bolt the leader clipped. If all that works, the leader falls twice the distance from the last clipped bolt. For example, if the leader climbs four feet higher than a bolt and falls, she will fall four feet back to the bolt and then another four feet before the rope jerks tight through that bolt. When the leader gets to the top of the climb, she runs the rope through belay anchors at the top and then lowers back down. The second climber is then on top-rope. The rope goes from the belayer, up through the anchors and back down to the climber. As the climber goes up, the belayer pulls in the rope through her belay device. That way, the climber on top-rope always has a tight rope and won't fall more than a few inches. Lead climbing is a bit more dangerous and way exciting because there is always fall potential. Also, you have to be able to let go with one hand to clip the carabiners at each bolt so it's harder to lead a climb than to second, or top-rope it. I think leading sounds very cool but I want to get better at just climbing before I start that.

"Have you belayed?" Jared asked.

"Well, sort of but not really. Sometimes when I went with just my dad, he would have me belay him off a tree or something because I was too small to actually catch him. We only did that on really easy climbs that he would never fall on so I kind of know how to belay, but I've never caught a fall."

Jared was quiet for a while. Apparently, he was trying to decide what to do with me.

"How about this," he offered. "We'll set up a top rope or two at the beginner's area just to get you off the ground and remind you how to belay. Then we'll head over to one of the gullies and I'll lead a couple of harder climbs for you. If I anchor you to the ground and have you use an auto-belay device, I'm sure you can catch me."

"Sounds great". Now I was getting pumped. We pulled into the parking lot, and I could feel my forearms pump and my hands sweat. No more thinking about Dad; no worries about making conversation with Jared. I was going climbing!

Jared walked to the back of the truck and handed me my pack. He then reached inside and started dragging gear towards the tailgate. He had enough stuff in there to climb El Capitan. He chose a pack and started sorting ropes and gear.

"I'm going to run to the bathroom," I said.

"Great."

I could see that I had plenty of time. When I returned, he was just closing up the truck and shouldered a massive pack. I slipped on my pack and headed towards the beginner's area. I was practically jogging to keep up with Jared's pace. He had been moving so slowly with everything else, I was unprepared for his sudden acceleration as we actually started moving towards the rock. The approach to the beginner's area was a pretty simple trail. We went down a gentle slope and then curved around and climbed back toward a ridge. In ten minutes, we were at the base of the climbs. Only one other party was set up. They had two ropes up which left about half a dozen climbs open. Jared dropped his pack and surveyed the available routes.

"Have you done any crack climbing?"

"Not much."

"How about *Bare Knuckles*? It sounds a little more burley than your other climbs."

"Okay."

"I'll scramble up over there and set up a top-rope. You can get your harness and shoes on and get ready to climb."

I had never actually climbed in this beginner's area. I don't know why, but Dad always took us to other parts of the park. The climbs here were pretty short, and most people just hiked up on the side like Jared was doing and set up the top-rope instead of leading the climb. I sat down and pulled stuff out of my pack. By the time I got my harness on, Jared was dropping a rope on the climb. I grabbed a drink and a snack to delay putting my shoes on. They're pretty tight and start to hurt if I wear them long. Jared was setting up a second rope on a nearby climb. I was starting to realize that guided climbing was going to mean a lot more climbing for me than the family outings I was used to. After waiting for Dad to lead a climb and taking turns with Mom and Walter, I was lucky if I got in two climbs in a day. We would probably pick off these two climbs in less than an hour. I hoped I could hold up for the whole day.

When Jared returned, I slipped on my shoes and stepped up to the first route.

"I know you've climbed some, but I'm going to go over all the safety stuff with you before you leave the ground."

"Okay."

"Do you know how to tie in?"

"Yes." He handed me the rope and I started to thread it

through my harness, which was a mistake because you actually have to start the knot first and then put the rope through. I realized my error and pulled it back through to start the knot. I worried that Jared was going to think I was completely clueless. I hadn't tied into a rope to climb for a couple of years, but I had tied in sometimes to play in the garage. We had this pulley hanging on the ceiling that Dad used to teach us how to belay. Sometimes I rigged up a rope swing there or tied into a rope and raised and lowered myself from the ceiling. I liked to pretend I was lowering off some big overhang. Anyway, I knew how to tie in, but I was struggling with my knot. Jared patiently pointed out my mistakes, and I got it right. He reviewed the belay signals and showed me how he would catch me if I fell and how I would lower from the top. Finally, I was ready to climb.

I stepped back and looked at the route. It was a small crack in a gentle corner. Climbers call it an open book. If the rock were a book, this one would be most of the way open with the crack right in the corner. That meant I could use hand and footholds on either side of the crack, and I could jam my hands and feet right into the crack to climb. I hadn't done much of that so at first, I tried to use the holds on the face and was struggling just to leave the ground.

"Try using the crack," Jared suggested. I got a toe into the crack and started to step up but didn't have any hand holds. I stepped down to the ground. Jared then showed me how to jam my fingers into the crack. I was about to try to go up again when a guy started to free solo up the rock right beside me. "Free" climbing means you don't use anything to get up but the rock. You don't pull on the rope or hang onto any gear. That's the climbing we usually do. If you pull on the rope or gear that would be "aid" climbing. "Solo" climbing means you do it alone. "Free solo" means climbing alone without a rope. If you fall, you hit the ground. My dad has strong feelings about free soloing. I think he lectured us every single time we went out to the rock about climbing without a rope. He always said that the little extra thrill was not worth the consequences of a fall (usually death). I really didn't need any convincing about that. I didn't even like to fall with a rope. No way would I free solo. Dad also had to tell us about all the good climbers who have died soloing easy routes to set up top ropes or who just fell off the top while setting up a rope. So, I was a little nervous watching this guy solo up beside me. Jared had me step back from the rock so I wouldn't be in the guy's landing zone if he decked. Jared looked a little peeved that the guy was soloing right over my head. Luckily, the guy moved away to set up his top-rope.

Finally, I got back to the climb. I made a couple of moves off the ground with my hands and feet in the crack. It worked, but I didn't feel very secure, and it was tough to balance with my hands and feet all in a vertical line. So as soon as I saw a little handhold on the face I grabbed that. Pretty soon I was halfway up and only had one foot still using the crack. I was getting a little more confident, but the climb was getting harder. I looked down and was amazed at how freaked I was at being off the ground. I turned back to face the rock and took a couple of breaths to try to relax. The footholds on the face were really small and to put both feet on the wall I had to press against the angle of the walls so that my feet were kind of pushing against each other. That's a move called "stemming" and it takes a bit of power and a lot of balance. It also meant that my legs were spread pretty far apart pushing out in opposite directions to try to push me up. Awkward and sketchy were the descriptions I had in mind. I could almost reach a decent handhold with my right fingers. I just needed to get a little bit higher. I wasn't sure my feet would even hold, but I had to move. I pressed out and down with both legs and stretched as far as I could with my right fingertips. I could just feel the edge of the hold when it happened. Right in the middle of the move, I farted. Not a big thunder roar, just a little umph. However, I knew that my butt with my legs spread wide was only a couple of feet over Jared's head. I was mortified. I didn't finish the reach I just froze for an instant. I was hoping like crazy that he wouldn't know what it was. Maybe he would think my shoe squeaked or something.

"Some people would call that aid." Okay, so he knew I farted. "But, I guess it's only aid if it helps you make the move, and you still haven't pulled that move," he said.

I lunged up to the hold and scrambled my feet back together in the crack.

"Free," I said. I pretty much cruised the rest of the climb using the crack and the holds on the face.

"Nice climb," said Jared when he had lowered me to the ground. "It's a 5.8, but by insisting on using the face instead of the crack you probably made it 5.9 or so."

Five-nine or so. I liked the sound of that. Not bad for a first climb. We moved to the next rope. This one was set up on a face climb. It was just a flat rock face that was about vertical and had little nubbins and tiny ledges for holds. This was more my type of climbing. The key was to find footholds to push you up and to just use hand holds to keep you balanced. Face climbing is mostly a thin balancing act for me, and I really like it.

Jared belayed me up the climb and barely gave me any advice. Once, when I moved my foot to a smaller hold to get my feet under me for balance, he said, "Nice move."

"I see we're in your element here," he said when he lowered me. "That was about 5.9. Let's get you ready to belay, and we'll go do some longer climbs like this in Hero Gully."

"Great."

"I'm going to tie you in to the ground and then set you up to belay me. I'll have you practice by belaying me on top-rope here. When we move to the gully, I'll show you the difference for belaying lead."

"Great."

Jared tied a piece of webbing to an exposed tree root and then attached it to my harness. He showed me how to hook up an auto belay device and then tied into the rope. He checked my harness and his knot and then had me check them.

"Does everything look okay?" he asked. It seemed like a trick question since he'd just checked everything, so I double checked.

"Don't you want your climbing shoes on?" I asked. It was the only thing I could think of.

"Not for this. I need to take a fall anyway so you can catch me." He smiled. "On belay?"

"Belay on," I answered.

"Climbing?"

"Climb on."

He went up about five feet and I gradually took in slack.

"Now pull it tight and lock it off and I'll sit back on the rope so you can feel my weight."

He sat back and the belay device locked off. His weight moved me slightly forward and pulled the webbing tight to the root. Once the webbing was tight, I really didn't feel any weight. Next, he went back up and had me leave about a foot of slack in the rope. This time he kind of jumped, and there was a brief jerk before everything locked off and caught him. He climbed back up and was talking to me about how to lower him when he jumped off without saying anything. I was surprised, but the system worked and caught him easily. So, he said I was ready to belay him on some easy leads. I took off my shoes and grabbed a snack and a drink while he hiked up to clean the ropes. I could get used to this guided climbing.

CHAPTER 13: MORE CLIMBER GUYS

I left my harness on and repacked my shoes and snacks. Jared shouldered his monster pack and led off toward the gully. We hiked for about 15 minutes through my favorite part of the park. A trail winds down to a stream, crosses on a small wooden bridge and then follows the stream through an aspen grove. The air is always so cool and sweet in the aspens, and the shimmering noise of their leaves is one of my favorite sounds in the world. I was glad that Jared wasn't a talkative hiker so I could listen to the leaves and the stream as we hiked along. When we came through the aspens the trail snaked up hill into an open area. We would pass the Barge Wall on the way to our gully. The Barge is a huge flat face covered in bolts. It has some really popular climbs on it and is always packed with climbers. It's practically a ritual for climbers hiking in to stop and talk with the groups hanging out at the Barge and we were sucked in right away.

"Hey Jared," came the first call as we drew near.

"Oh look, it's Katie Brown," someone else said. Jared looked at me, and I just shook my head. I figured everyone would know him, but I didn't expect to see anyone who would know me (okay, so they didn't know my name, but they recognized me). I looked over to see a whole pack of guys from the Ravine hanging around a couple of top-ropes on the Barge.

"Alright Jared, we thought you'd be out guiding one of your little rich clients, but you get to actually climb today huh?"

I stared at Jared practically ordering him to say I wasn't a client.

"Yeah," he said. "Great day for it."

"Yeah, and *Jack Face* was open can you believe it? We never climb here cuz it's always taken. Hey, you guys want a ride before we pull the rope?"

Jared stared at me practically ordering me to say no.

I was so torn. This could be my chance. If I did a climb with the guys, I might get invited out with them again. If I blew them off, maybe not. If I said yes, Jared might say I couldn't cuz I was a client. I had heard of *Jack Face*. I thought it was pretty hard but it looked like the kind of face climb I would have a chance at. I looked back at Jared. He was ready to move on down the trail. Clearly, I had to say no.

"Sure," I said. "I'll give it a try." I dropped my pack and started digging out my shoes, careful not to look up at Jared. He seemed to stand there thinking for a while, then dropped his pack and walked over to Tyler who had just belayed the last climber. I busied myself pulling on my shoes. When I walked up to the rope, Jared had taken over the belay.

"Thanks," I whispered. I chalked my hands and scoped out the route. It was a very steep, flat face with tiny edges for holds and an occasional little pocket that would take a couple of fingers. Oh crap I thought, I might not even get off the ground. I had to make myself breathe while I tied into the rope. Then, I chalked my hands again and tried to take a couple more slow breaths while I looked at the first moves. The Ravine guys were repacking and lounging about and talking with other climbers. Fortunately, they weren't all focusing on my start. Jared pointed out some starting holds and we exchanged commands.

"On belay?"

"Belay on."

"Climbing."

"Climb on...don't fart." Fortunately, he whispered the last part. Just what I needed to boost my confidence as I started a climb in front of the guys.

I stepped up on the first little holds and immediately moved up to the next. Each hold was so tiny I could only hang on it for a short time. When I was sure I was falling off one hold, I'd shift my weight to the next. Almost immediately, I'd feel like I was falling from that hold, and I'd have to move again.

"Use your feet," said Jared.

I made slow steady progress up the route. I started to relax at about 15 feet because I figured I was past the point of pure humiliation if I fell. At least I'd made part of the climb. A couple moves higher I came to a place where I clearly had to traverse to the left. I had my right hand directly in front of my chest and I had to reach way over and up with my left.

"Nice work Katie! You need to gaston there."

"I don't know Gaston," I replied through clenched teeth. "All I can do is this..." I used my right hand to pull myself to the left like I was opening a sliding door. It didn't feel like I would stay on the rock throughout the move. Even the slightest breeze would have tossed me backwards and down. But, I stuck. I reached the hold with my left hand and shuffled my feet over and up.

"Nice work. Now you know Gaston."

"Whatever," I thought. I just had to focus totally to stay on the rock in the new spot. I could see that I was at the last big move. Everything so far had been really balancy. Now I had to pull one hard move up and back to the right. I secured my left handhold and moved my left foot up just below it. My right foot was on a tiny nubbin directly below me, but it couldn't really hold any weight. I was just hoping to rest the weight of my right leg on it. I had to push up totally with my left leg and use my left arm to keep me on the rock. Then I had to stretch way up and right with my right hand to a pretty big ledge.

Slowly, I powered up with my leg and stretched up my right hand. Closer, closer, I could feel the edge of the hold but couldn't quite stretch my fingers over it. I lowered back down and tried to catch my breath. However, there was no way to relax with my left hand and foot doing all the work. I knew I had to get this move quickly or come off. I powered back up, got to just the same place, then tried to stretch up taller.

I was in the air without warning. My left foot popped and my right foot didn't even slow me down. My left hand was still pulling when my feet popped and ripped me to the left as I took to the air. I only fell about a foot and was more frustrated than scared. The nice thing about falling on steep rock is that you usually just hang in the air. I shook my hands out, grabbed a hold in front of my face and pulled back onto the rock. I had to make one move to get back to my previous spot.

"Nice try. I think you'll have to lunge for it this time."

"Dyno, Katie Brown."

Gaston, Dyno, Lunge, I just wanted to climb. I reached my high point and secured my left hand. I moved my left foot a little higher then squatted as low onto that leg as I could with my left hand hanging out straight. I took a slow breath and then powered up, this time driving up as high as I could while reaching up in the same motion. I was going to catch that hold or fly past it. This was a one-shot effort. At the very top of the movement I put my hand to the rock and latched onto the hold. My left hand and right foot came loose, and I swung a little to the right. I just barely stayed on until I could find a right foot hold and then I stood up. I heard cheers from below as I pulled a couple more, easier moves and touched the anchors.

"I'm there," I said with my last ounce of breath.

"Nice job. Lean back and I'll lower you." Jared eased me back to the ground and pulled some slack through the rope.

"Nice climb. That looked tough. I can reach past a couple of those gnarly moves you had to make." I didn't look up to see which one of the guys was talking. I was trying to untie my knot but my hands were so tired and shaky that I wasn't getting anywhere. Jared reached up and loosened it for me.

"Thanks again," I said quietly.

"Nice job."

Finally, I freed myself from the rope.

"We're headed for the upper gorge," said Tyler. "You guys want to come along."

Jared didn't hesitate this time. "No, we're headed to Hero Gully. Thanks for the climb though."

"Sure. Have a good one."

"See you later," I said as we shouldered our packs. "Thanks for the ride."

We headed off towards the Gully as the guys loudly deserted the Barge and moved off towards the Upper Gorge. The voices trailed off as we rounded a bend.

"So, I guess I should have talked to you about guiding and climbing with other groups. Technically, I'm supposed to decide what you should try, and I'm supposed to set up any climb that you do."

We walked in silence for a bit, then Jared continued. "Since I hadn't said anything to you when we started, and since it was a clean set up and I could belay you, I figured we could get away with it this once. No more though, okay?"

I turned to look at him. I couldn't hold back the grin that spread from ear to ear.

"Thank you," I said. "That was so cool. That was so fun. I can't believe I almost made that climb. I'm so glad you didn't tell them you were guiding me. Thank you. I see those guys at the Ravine, and they talk about bringing me out here. I really wanted to show them that I could climb. Did I climb alright? Did I look like I knew what I was doing?"

Now Jared couldn't help but crack a little smile. "Yeah. You looked okay. You tied your knot right and nobody heard you fart."

"I didn't fart."

"Getting that dyno move was pretty sweet. Next time you'll have to get it without a fall. I think that pitch is rated 5.10b."

"No way."

He just kept walking.

"10b. No way. I was so close."

"Well, let's get on a couple of climbs that you can make today, and then you can start to crank up the numbers."

I was so pumped.

We got to the Gully and Jared set me up to belay him while he led a couple of 5.9s. There was no way he would fall on a 5.9, but I was a little nervous on the belay. I was not looking forward to catching my first leader fall. I was very relieved when he set up the top ropes and rapped down. I made both climbs without too much trouble. Jared had me do them each twice so he could coach me on some of the moves. I gotta say, I learned a lot that way. Sometimes a little change in my position made a huge difference in how hard a move was. And he kept pointing out that I was squeezing the rock too hard. He constantly had me change my balance trying to get me to work with the rock, and every time he told me to breathe (and he told me a lot), I found that I wasn't breathing. By the end of the second lap on the second route, I was toast. We finished our snacks and reviewed the climbs. He offered to set up one more but suggested we should probably call it a day. I had no trouble agreeing. I felt great about the day and was exhausted.

Jared talked more on the hike out than he had all day. He talked about routes that were similar to the ones we did and about other routes because they were different. He suggested that I work on cracks and stemming and just keep bouldering a lot. He said the guys I knew from the Ravine were good, safe climbers and that I'd probably be okay climbing with them but probably shouldn't belay the big guys. He also said I shouldn't count on an invitation. Climbers can be a little selfish about their climbing time, and they might not want to take a chance with someone so young.

We tossed our packs in his truck and headed towards town. A few miles down the road, Jared seemed to run out of words again. He stuck in a CD. Rap. I was surprised. I hadn't thought about Jared's musical tastes, but I usually climbed with Dad and there was no chance of rap music playing in his truck. That, of course, started me missing Dad and I was off on one of my daydreams when I realized we had pulled into a gas station/deli.

"I need a burrito," said Jared as he hopped out of the truck. "Want anything?"

The timing was horrible. I was just sitting there missing Dad, and we pulled into the same gas station where he always stopped after climbing. Apparently, this place was some kind of climbers' tradition.

"Dad likes this...." I got choked up in mid sentence. Jared was opening the tailgate and I started to dig through my pack. I tried to turn away from Jared so he wouldn't see my tears. He put his hand on mine.

"I'll get this," he said. "What would you like?"

"Veggie burrito, Coke," I choked out. He walked away, and I closed the tailgate. I wasn't going to just stand there and cry. I went into the gas station restroom and washed my hands and face. I climbed back into the truck just before Jared. He handed me my food and unwrapped his burrito.

"Tell your dad you did good today. He'd be proud."

This was not helpful. We ate in silence for a few minutes.

"You know those things I kept telling you about climbing today?"

"Yeah?" I didn't really know what he was talking about.

"I find them helpful for a lot of situations." He slid a map off the dashboard and pointed to a scrap of paper stuck underneath. It was a quote by a climber named Susan Fox Rogers. It said:

...it is through climbing that I learned the most important lessons in life. Hold on, but not too tight; work with the rock, don't fight it; balance is everything; and always remember to breathe.

I laughed as I read the last line because, once again, I wasn't breathing.

"That's good," I said. "I'll work on it."

I finished my burrito as we drove. I went over the climbs in my head. One of the cool things about climbing (at least for someone who daydreams like me) is that I can enjoy the climbs for days afterwards. I replayed each move, felt the pressure on fingers and toes, the balance and the power. Next thing I knew we were pulling into my driveway.

Jared handed me my pack from the back of the truck, and I thanked him. He said, "Nice job. See you on the rock."

"Great," I said. "Thanks."

CHAPTER 14: A PLAN IS FORMED

Turning towards the house with my pack over my shoulder, I suddenly felt all the fatigue of the day. My legs could barely hold me. I had been hoping to sit in the kitchen and review the whole day with Dad play by play. Now I felt tired and sweaty, and really just wanted a bath.

I walked through the house to dump my pack in the garage. Mom and Dad were sitting at the table. It was dinner time. I hadn't even thought about that when I got the burrito.

"Hey babe, we didn't know if you'd be home in time for supper, do you want me to set a place for you?"

"No thanks Mom, I had a burrito on the way home."

"Taco Stand?" asked Dad with a smile.

"Yup."

"How was it?"

"Delicious as always."

"I meant the climbing."

I paused. Words were not going to be sufficient to describe how much I had enjoyed the day.

"Great," I offered.

"What did you climb?"

"We started on the Beginners Wall." I dropped my pack on the floor and slumped onto a stool at the kitchen bar. I described each climb, the 10b with one fall and the clean 5.9s. Dad was appropriately interested and impressed.

"Was Jared alright to hang out with? If I remember right, he's a little quiet. I think he's a poet or philosopher or something."

"Yeah, he was cool. He let me do the one climb with some other climbers." I couldn't really explain to Dad that they were guys I knew from the Ravine without admitting to a lot of time out there on my own. "And he gave me some really helpful tips."

"Great. I guess we need to find a way to get you out there more often."

"Definitely." The conversation kind of stalled there. "Man, I've got to clean up." I took my pack to the garage and headed for the bath.

Every scratch and scrape from every climb lit up as I submerged my body into the water. Soon however, the warm water relaxed my muscles and I floated into a deep, soft state of satisfaction. "Satisfying" was my dad's word for a good climb. He said a roller coaster ride could be fun and exciting like a climb, but it could never satisfy the way a climb can. Lying there in the hot water feeling every muscle I had used, I felt completely satisfied with my day. For about 5 minutes. Then I started to think about what I could do to get that 5.10b climb without falling. I would find a place to practice that long reach and be ready for it next time I got to the park.

Eventually, I forced myself to drain the tub and get out. I pulled on some clean sweats and headed to the living room. Mom, Dad and Walter were in the middle of a discussion. I plopped onto the couch and listened.

"Jack will be back in a game or two. It's a hip pointer, which I guess is a bad bruise. Really painful, but he should be okay. Meanwhile, they're pulling Cory into Jack's spot and Davis will take the outside linebacker spot most of the time. He's big and strong but not too quick. It looks like I could get in on every long yardage play and maybe some others. This could be my best chance cuz Jack might be back next week." Walter was pumped. As much as I resented all the football focus since Dad's injury, I had no trouble getting excited for Walter.

"That's great honey," said Mom. But she seemed to be troubled. "It's just that the next game is at Collinwood. That's one of the longest road trips you have."

"It is the longest. We're going to spend the night and come home Saturday. Sure wish you could be there."

Mom and Dad looked at each other. It was like they had an entire conversation without saying a word. Walter and I sat and waited to see how their silent conversation would come out.

"Maybe I could go," said Mom when they finally broke from their gaze. "Joan and I have talked about a road trip. We could see the game, stay in a hotel, do a little shopping."

"Cuz what's football without a little shopping?" joked Dad. "I think that's a great plan. I don't think I'm ready for a football/ shopping road trip just yet, but I'd like it if you could be there."

Dad looked at me. "Think the two of us could stay out of trouble if they leave us unattended for a weekend?"

"It's a chance they'll have to take," I smiled. I leaned back on the couch and thought about how nice it would be to get to hang out with just Dad. I enjoyed that thought for about a minute, then I started plotting. This could be my chance to get him away from the TV. A hike? The park? The Ravine? What would it be? I needed to coax him into the woods and make sure he had a good time so he would come back. I began to consider the possibilities in great detail. I imagined the two of us in all the different locations, weather conditions, activities. Apparently, I was at it for a while because when I next looked around the room, I was the only one there. I may look spacey, but I'm usually very busy when I drift away.

I decided the Ravine was the best shot. It's close to town and I could show him how I was doing on the rock. He could coach me through some moves, and he might see some of his old climber friends. We could drive out in his truck. If we took the long approach, he could avoid the death drop I try to ride on my Mt bike, and he could roll right up to the rock. Also, it's way out in the woods, so he could remember how much he likes the wilderness. I had my destination. Now my plan. I was pretty sure that Mom and Walter would not approve of me dragging Dad out into the woods. So, I plotted in secret. I thought I was acting pretty nonchalant about Mom and Walter going away but Walter must have picked up on something. That, or he just knew that I would try something once they were out of the way. Thursday night he actually came into my room to talk to me. I don't think he had stepped foot inside my room in two years.

"What's up?" I tried to be casual.

"So, you got plans for the weekend?" Walter got right to the point.

"Yeah, I think we'll go for a picnic or something."

"Sounds nice. Where do you plan to picnic? Top of Polar Bear Spire?"

"Come on, I'm not going to try to get Dad to do anything stupid. We'll just drive to a park or something and picnic by his truck."

Walter eyed me suspiciously for a moment. "Well, be nice. Don't spend the whole weekend lecturing him about watching TV."

I didn't really want to have this conversation, so I tried to change the subject. "So, will you get to play quite a bit tomorrow?"

Walter's eyes lit up right away. This was almost too easy.

"Yeah, coach is going to play me in all the long yardage situations and, if Davis misses even one tackle, I might get in on a lot more plays. Coach says I'm really too small and the running backs usually fall forward for a few yards when I tackle them, but since I have good form and wrap every tackle, he is confident that I won't do any harm."

"Well, there's a vote of confidence."

"Yeah, he said that I have to keep making sure tackles and never go for the big hit. He says if I ever go for the big hit and the running back stays up, he'll pull me for the rest of the game. And Davis is big and knocks people backwards, but he never wraps them up. If their running back breaks through a couple of Davis's tackles, I could be in."

"Awesome."

"Yeah, well, as long as I don't go for the big hit."

"Of course you won't.....right?"

Walter just smiled at me for a bit. "Not unless it can be a really big hit."

He started out the door and was into the hallway before he remembered that he had come in to lecture me.

He leaned back into my room. "Don't forget. Be nice."

"Wrap them up," I answered.

Later, I talked to Dad about how we could spend our time together. We agreed that we would do something special on Friday after school. He was thinking dinner and a movie. When Mom and Walter got ready for their road trip, I told Dad I wanted to have a picnic dinner with him. That way, he would be prepared to be outside somewhere, and I wouldn't spring the location on him until we were on our way. I told him to be ready to roll by 3:00 when school let out. He got into it right away. He didn't have therapy on Friday, so he prepared the picnic while I was in school. I packed my backpack the same as I did on my bouldering days, so I had my shoes and chalk bag ready to go.

CHAPTER 15: THE PLAN IN ACTION

Friday morning, we said goodbye to Mom and Walter. Mom was excited but nervous about leaving Dad. She kept reminding him of things he needed to take care of, and she reviewed all of his needs. She gave him a list of people he could call if he needed any assistance. He told her to drive carefully and assured her that he would call for help if needed.

I was just pumped. I can't say I learned much at school that day. I was even more spacey than usual. I kept checking the weather out the window. It was a pretty nice day with big, broken clouds in a bright blue sky. The wind was a little strong, but I didn't figure that would bother us down in the Ravine unless it blew in a rainstorm. When the final bell rang, I was totally ready to roll. I zipped home on my bike and threw my pack in the back of Dad's truck. He took forever to get the picnic together but finally we headed out to the truck. He slid into the driver's seat, and I folded his wheelchair and put it in the back. I climbed in beside him and off we went. We were at the edge of our neighborhood before he even asked where we were going.

"Well, which way?"

"Head left."

"And then?"

"I thought maybe we could drive out by the Ravine where we

used to boulder."

Dad looked over at me then back at the road. Time ticked slowly by. I looked at people in the passing cars. I didn't want to say anything because I was afraid I'd sound like I was trying to trick him into something."

"It's been a while since I've been out there," he finally responded. "A picnic, huh?" he smiled. He was on to me. "I don't suppose you have your climbing shoes tucked away in that backpack?"

"Well, you know, just in case."

"Good. This will be good. You should get to do some bouldering. I haven't had much chance to get you out there this year."

That's because you've been sitting on the couch or watching Walter's football practices, I wanted to say. But luckily, my better judgment came through and I stayed quiet. I needed to focus on having success today. No arguing, just have some fun so he would want to do it again.

"I don't have to do much," I said. "I thought I might show you a couple of problems I've been working on." Dad pulled that move again where he glanced over at me and then back at the road. He never was one to talk without thinking about it first.

"So, you've gotten out there recently?"

"Oh, a couple of times," I tried to sound casual. "I rode out there on my bike after school."

Another brief silence.

"Did you head out through the old apple orchard?"

"Yeah."

"That's a sweet ride isn't it."

I couldn't hold back anymore. "It's so cool. I love the series of whoops just as you launch into the woods. Coming back is the greatest though. It's just enough downhill that you can really cruise but not so steep as to be scary." We were both smiling now, remembering the curves and the bumps.

"You know, I don't want you to ride out there anymore unless you tell us when you're going. I don't even want you that far into the woods without knowing when and where you are."

"You think Mom will let me go?"

"Do you have any friends you could go with?"

"Not really, but I've gotten to know the regulars down there pretty well."

"In a couple of times out?"

"Well, I might have gone a few times."

"I'll work on your mom."

"Thanks Dad."

Dad slowed the truck as we reached the fire road turn off. The road wasn't in too bad of shape because they were doing some logging near the Ravine and had recently bulldozed it. Still, it had some big ruts and rocks. I was concerned about how he would manage to balance his body in the rocking truck and still control the truck with hand controls. The first big rut tipped the truck sideways and tossed Dad into the door. As the truck climbed up out of the rut, the truck leveled off and Dad slid back into his seat. He stopped the truck and took his hands off the controls.

Oh crap, I thought. He's not going to be able to do this with the hand controls.

I watched him reach up and pull the shoulder strap all the way out. Then he let it back in and snugged it up against his chest. That locked the belt tight and held Dad in place. He looked at me and smiled and said, "Hang on."

What was I worried about? He was going to love this challenge. Half a mile later he was cruising us through the bumps and ruts like he'd been doing this all his life. I was so pumped. We were in the woods, and he was having a good time.

"It's been a while," he said as we pulled up near the Ravine. The pullout where people parked had also been bulldozed for the logging operation. There was only one other vehicle in sight. The front fender of an old beater car was embedded halfway into a sage bush. It looked like the driver had hopped out before he finished parking.

"Hey look, a handicapped parking spot." Dad pulled up to the side of the clearing where the bulldozer had recently expanded the pullout. There was a large flat area that extended right up to the trees. In fact, roots of a big ponderosa were exposed along the edge, right where Dad stopped the truck. I looked up at the towering pine.

"You don't suppose that's about to topple over?" asked Dad.

"Hope not."

"I'm thinkin' that if it falls it'll go the other way. The roots on the other side are still good. They should keep it up. Without these it seems that it would fall away from us. Anyway, it'll probably last another hundred years if they don't cut it."

"Works for me." I hopped out of the truck and walked to the back to get Dad's chair. He had picked the spot because it had such a nice flat area to put the chair beside his door. I bristled at the "handicapped" comment. He slid out easily and we both looked around.

"Maybe we should picnic here and then maybe I can show you the stuff I'm working on."

"Works for me," said Dad. I dropped the tailgate and set up our picnic. Dad rolled up to it like a table while I sat on the tailgate beside the food. It was a pretty measly picnic with a couple sandwiches and some chips, but it was, after all, just an excuse to be here, and I think we both knew that. The wind fought us for every bite. I had to weight down the paper products with rocks. Dad had baked some chocolate chip cookies, and they made it seem like a special meal. Just as we were breaking out the cookies a couple of the guys came hiking up out of the Ravine. One of them I recognized. He had often been there when I bouldered.

"Hey, Katie Brown!" He yelled across the lot. "What no bike today?" Dad gave me a funny look but didn't say anything. Then the guy saw Dad. "Hey, Jeff, right?"

"Yeah," said Dad.

"Hey, it's good to see you. You doing alright?"

"Yeah," said Dad.

"Hey, is she yours?" the guy said, motioning towards me.

"Yeah," said Dad.

"So that's where she gets it. She's been tearing this place up. Sending everything in sight. Yeah."

"Cool," said Dad.

"Well, hey, see ya."

"Yeah," said Dad. We watched as the climbers piled into their car and rolled away.

"Hey," said Dad. "Katie Brown?"

"I don't know. Some of the guys call me that when I come down here. I don't think they actually know who I am."

"Well, hey, you could be called a lot worse."

"Yeah." I looked at him and we both cracked up.

"Hey," I said. "Want another cookie?"

"I think I'm done.

"Yeah?" I said, and took the last cookie. We packaged up the picnic stuff and threw it in the cab. I reached into the truck and grabbed my backpack.

"Can you reach my gloves there?" Dad asked. He wears these fingerless bike gloves when he goes any distance in his chair. They give him better grip and keep his hands from getting all torn up. He was definitely going to need them out here. I tossed the gloves to Dad and shouldered my pack. We headed for the Ravine.

"I think if we take the upper trail to the other side of the Ravine, the approach will be less harsh."

"You mean you want to avoid the 'death drop'?"

"Yeah," I said. We started across the upper trail.

"Have you ever tried the death drop on your bike?"

I was really glad he asked cuz I was pretty proud of it but didn't want to brag. "Yeah, I got so that I can usually make it."

He looked at me again. "So, you've been down here a couple of times and you have a nickname and you've learned to ride the death drop?"

"Well, maybe more than a couple."

We reached the part of the trail that descends into the Ravine. I was pretty nervous about Dad managing this stretch of trail.

It's no death drop, but it is a bit steep and bumpy.

Dad didn't even hesitate. He picked his line and cruised down the trail. At the bottom he spun around to look at the rock face. He looked happy to be here, and I was ecstatic. I was at the rock with my dad. The Ravine sheltered us from the wind. We could hear it ripping overhead, but only a light breeze reached us.

"So, what can you do here?"

"Well, I've ticked off the main traverse and a couple of little problems on the other side. Then I've done *Urban Guerrilla...*"

"You've pulled the *Guerrilla*?"

"Yeah, it took a while, but I've got it pretty wired."

"Awesome. Let's see it."

I dropped my pack and pulled out my shoes. The *Guerrilla* was a traversing problem that pulled over a big overhang. Most of the guys just let their feet hang out into space and crank serial pull-ups to get through the problem. I could never pull that many pull-ups, so I found some small foot holds and sometimes threw a heel hook to use my legs to hold my body up while I moved my hands out the overhang. I chalked up and cruised the problem for Dad. He was very supportive. He said he was impressed with my footwork and strength. That was all very cool, but I wanted to really show him something.

"So Dad, after I got *Urban Guerrilla*, I started looking for a route up this side that didn't pull the overhang. I started to work a low route up this side. I only worked on it when no one was around. It was all dirty, and I was sure no one had ever climbed it before. It's the hardest thing I've ever done, and the only thing I've done without knowing what it was. I worked on it a bunch. I had even picked out a name for it, I was going to call it *The Lowdown.*

"Well, the day I was ready to get the whole problem there were a bunch of guys here. I got on it anyway cuz I was sure I was going to make it. No one was paying any attention to me. But just as I got to the crux one of the guys said ..."

"*SqueezePlay.*"

I looked over at Dad. "You know the problem? So did they.

They started giving me advice. I was so bummed, I thought I invented it. And *Squeeze Play*. Come on. What a stupid name. That's a baseball term. This is climbing. Don't you think that name sucks?"

"Well, *The Low Down* would have been good too. Let's see you do it."

Squeeze Play was still kind of hard for me, but I just barely made it and again, Dad seemed happy.

"Well, this is probably getting a little boring for you," I said. "Should we head back to the truck?"

"No way. We still have a little time before it gets dark. Let me show you a couple of other obscure problems."

"Great."

Dad rolled a little ways along the wall. He stopped between two problems I knew. Whatever he planned to show me must be obscure. I had never seen anyone going up in that spot. A little to the left was a flake that people sometimes tried to get to, but it was pretty high, and I had never seen anyone reach it. He stared at the wall in silence and then broke into a smile.

"Tom and I spent an entire afternoon laying siege to this spot. By the time we figured out the sequence, we were too spent to climb it. We came back the next day and Tom sent it on his first try. I think I got it on my third. We were all excited about it but no one else seemed to enjoy it so much. Part of the problem is that you dyno up to that fragile flake and about every other time you grab for it, a piece breaks off. It can be a nasty fall."

"Where does it start?"

Dad pointed to a little crease about eight inches off the ground. Then he picked up a couple pebbles from the ground and tossed them up to show me the initial hand holds. One was a little hole you could stick one finger into. The other was a small, horizontal crack. From there, if I could get there, it looked like I would move my right hand up to a small vertical hold and then go way up left to a ledge with my left hand. It looked much farther than I could ever reach.

I stepped up to the rock and tried to pull the first move. I didn't even get off the ground. I chalked my hands and looked at it for a while then tried again. And again. On about my fourth try I got my balance right and made it onto the initial holds. I reached up to the crack with my right hand and then leaned way left to try for the ledge. Not even close. I hopped back down.

Dad smiled. "That's the spot that stopped us for so long. As long as you have that right hand, you won't be able to reach the ledge with your left. But, if you let go of the right, you'll peel off the rock in an instant."

"Yeah, I see that."

"Want some beta?" That was his way of asking if I want him to tell me how to do it. It's some climber expression I've never understood.

"Yeah."

"See that little flake to the right? It's just beyond where your right knee will be when you're back on the rock."

"Yeah."

"Well, you can hook your right toe behind it just enough to hold you in to the rock. Then, let yourself fall to the left and grab the ledge just before you come off."

I looked to see if he was joking. He was still looking at the rock like he was watching someone do the move. What could I do? I had to try it. The first time I hooked my toe but didn't trust it at all. I kind of leaned left and then let go with my right hand. I knew I was going to fall and half-heartedly threw up my left hand as I was coming off. It raked the ledge just as I cut loose! Wow, this could really work.

I got back on. This time I focused on that ledge as I let myself fall left. I got the ledge and just managed to stop my fall. I moved both feet under me to the horizontal crack I'd first used as a hand hold. This had me fully extended, tiptoes on the crack, fingertips on the ledge.

"Awesome," said Dad. "Now from there we just had to dyno, jump to that thin flake. But don't try it, it's too far of a fall and parts of the flake often break."

There was no way I could jump up from my stretched out

position. You have to bend your legs a little to jump and mine were stretched out straight. Instead, I looked for something to step up to. There wasn't much. No wonder they jumped from here. If I were 6 inches taller, I would probably have jumped too. Eventually, I found a small divot in the rock and smeared against it with my left foot. It was pretty high, up near my waist. Slowly, I placed my right foot beside it. I knew they wouldn't hold much. I locked my right hand onto the ledge and slowly extended my left. Gradually, I put some weight on my feet expecting to pop off any second. Little by little I went up. My left hand got closer to the flake. I didn't breathe or even blink. I was getting too high off the ground but so close to the flake that I couldn't stop. Finally, I locked my left hand onto the flake. Just as I lifted my right hand, my foot popped off the wall. I grabbed for the flake with my right hand as my other foot popped swinging me into space. I hung from the flake with my hands while my feet swung out and then back to the wall. I scraped around trying to find some place to step. My right hand suddenly swung free with a crack of the rock. I was hanging from one arm! I dropped the broken rock from my right hand and grabbed another place on the flake. I found a slight hold for one foot and traversed left. Soon I had both feet on and my hands were on a more solid piece of the flake. Now I tried to catch up on breathing. My heart was pounding so hard I was afraid the thump, thump, thump would knock me off the wall.

"From there you just keep moving left. It keeps getting easier until you can just walk off the far end of the rock." Dad's voice snapped me back from space. I traversed to the edge of the rock. The ledges were covered with dirt and sand, so I had to move very cautiously even though the holds were good. I hopped onto the trail at the edge of the rock and walked back down to Dad.

He was smiling and shaking his head. "I didn't mean for you to actually do it," he said. "I just wanted to show you the first moves."

"I didn't mean to do it. It just sort of came together."

"Nice climb! Really though, don't go that high without a

spotter and a crash pad."

I looked back at the climb. Whoa, it was up there. "Okay. Cool problem. What's it called?"

Dad hesitated. "You won't like this one either. We called it *Homerun* because of the huge jump and grab that we used. You just walked up there. Nice climbing."

"Thanks."

"That's the problem with a lot of the climbs here; they go so high. Have you worked any problems in the next gully over? The Tick Ranch?"

"No," I said. "I've heard about it, but I've never even looked over there."

Dad looked at the darkening sky and at the trail. "Let's see if I can get over there. I'll just show you a couple of things you can work on some time."

CHAPTER 16: THE PLAN FALLS APART

This was so cool. Dad was getting into it. Everything I could have hoped for was falling into place. I was climbing well, Dad was having a good time, and he was getting around well. I didn't care if it was stormed and we stayed out all night. I was totally pumped.

I helped Dad a little on the trail up out of the Ravine. He really did pretty well with it. The trail to Tick Ranch was more obscure. But Dad got pretty good at bumping over exposed roots and rocks. The wind blasted us on the higher part of the trail, but soon we descended into another gully and found some shelter. The rock here was not as tall but it was less featured and just a little steeper than vertical. I thought this would fit my strengths pretty well, but Dad pointed out a couple of problems and I never really got off the ground on either of them. He was cool about it. I think we were both still a little shocked that I had done *Homerun*.

By the time Dad got done showing me routes I was toast. I didn't actually do much climbing because it was all so hard, I never made more than one move before coming off. But my fingertips were shredded and filthy, and the light was almost gone.

"I guess we should try to find the truck before it's completely dark," Dad finally suggested. There was no way I was going to be the first one to say we should go. But it was clearly time.

"Yeah," I answered. Then I stopped and looked him in the eyes. "Thanks for coming out Dad. I had so much fun."

"Me too. Dang, I can't believe how well you're climbing."

"Thanks, but did you have fun? Or was it a pain coming all the way out here just for me?"

"First of all. I'd come out here just for you anytime, and it would be great because I'd be with you. And secondly, I love it out here...." Just then a big gust of wind blew a bunch of dust and leaves in our faces. "...even in the dark in a storm," he finished.

I rubbed the dust out of my eyes. "Me too. But let's get out of here."

The darkness really closed in on us as we made our way back towards the truck. I listened to the wind howling through the treetops. It seemed that you could hear a big gust coming from miles away, getting louder and louder until it slammed into us. We moved up the trail to a fire road and turned towards the parking area.

Suddenly we both stopped. Something had changed. I wasn't sure what it was. It was like part of the wind noise was suddenly missing. I looked at Dad. He had his head cocked to the side listening for something. Next I heard, and kind of felt, a ripping. The only description I could think of was like a large tree being ripped out of the ground. I could almost feel the ground being torn open. More sounds joined in. Branches were cracking and falling. Then, at almost the same time, came a tremendous crash and a thud that shook the earth. Literally. I grabbed Dad's chair to steady myself. If you've ever been in an earthquake, you know the sickening, disorienting feeling that comes with the earth moving. When something that can't happen happens, you begin to lose touch with what's real and what's not. You doubt everything and need something to hang on to. Something you can really count on. I turned to Dad.

Dad looked up at me with the strangest smile on his face. "It's just possible that my theory about the tree roots was wrong."

Oh my gosh. The truck. Did the tree really fall on the truck? We both started moving again. I couldn't decide if I wanted to run ahead and look, or hold back for fear of what I might see.

When we finally pulled into the clearing, it took me a while to realize what I was looking at. The clearing was essentially gone. It was now pretty much filled with the huge ponderosa pine. The tree had fallen and extended clear across the parking area and into the woods on the other side. Even though the tree was lying on the ground, branches stuck up 15 or 20 feet into the air. We couldn't see over the tree in the middle of the parking area. Over on the side by Dad's truck it was a different story. The trunk had no branches there. The front of his truck was looking up at a funny angle. The tree trunk had hit just behind the cab. It had smashed the back part of the cab, and the windows were broken out. The front of the bed was pinned close to the ground. The truck was nearly severed in half. Dad's truck. He loved that truck. I was afraid to look at him. He was going to be devastated.

Then, right next to me, I heard the strangest sound. Laughter. I looked over to Dad. He was hysterical. He was looking at his truck and laughing like it was the funniest thing he'd ever seen. I looked back at the truck and the tree. It was kind of funny looking. Soon we were both at it.

"Yup, those roots on the other side will probably hold it up for another hundred years," I tried to imitate his voice.

"If it does fall. It will certainly fall the other way," Dad joined in making fun of his predictions. Soon though we were both silent. I think we were both starting to realize our predicament. I watched as Dad reached into the pack on his chair to get his cell phone. Then I watched his face drop as he pulled the tv remote out of the pack. His cell phone was probably on the coffee table in front of the TV.

"Dad?"

"Yeah?"

"Have I ever mentioned that I should have my own cell phone?"

"About a million times."

"And I told you it would be useful and help keep me safe?"

"Uh huh."

"This is just the type of situation that I was concerned about."

Dad looked over at me. "You thought you needed a cell phone in case a tree ever fell on my truck?"

"You know. Any kind of unpredictable accident that might leave me stranded."

"Is this your way of saying 'I told you so'?"

"I'm just saying, you should take me more seriously when I ask for stuff."

"I'll try to keep that in mind."

We both looked around in the dark. It was a long way back to the main road, and a longer way back to town. I looked at the tree again. I didn't think we could get Dad's chair around it to get on the fire road if we were to try to hike out.

"What do we do?" I said out loud without really planning to.

There was a moment of silence, and I started to get very anxious.

"When was the last time you and I camped out?" said Dad.

I just looked at him. He couldn't be serious. We didn't have a tent. He was in a wheelchair for goodness sake. But there he sat, looking around, making plans for a campout. There was no fighting it. Our fate was sealed. We were sleeping in the woods tonight.

"Wienie Roast Rock?" I asked. There was a huge rock a little ways back on the fire road that was overhanging on one side. There was a fire pit part way under the overhang and, apparently, somebody had roasted wienies there once because everyone knew it by name. It provided some shelter from the wind and maybe a little protection if it rained. It seemed the obvious place to try to set up camp.

"That should work," said Dad.

"But no hot dogs," I said remembering my recent pukage. Then I thought of Dad. "Can you really stay out here all night?" I asked. "What about going to the bathroom? Can you sleep on the ground?"

"I have two catheters in the truck. That should be enough if I don't drink any more water and we get out of here pretty early in the morning. Tomorrow is Saturday, so there are sure to be some climbers coming in. I won't have to poop till late morning, so I'll be okay with that. I've been practicing "floor transfers" in therapy. That's getting from the floor to my chair. So I guess it's time to try it in the real world.

"Let's gather up everything we can from the truck and go set up at Wienie Roast Rock." He looked at the fallen tree for a moment. "Let's cut some small branches from that tree and use them to pad a bed. Normally, we wouldn't cut up branches to sleep on, but I think when a tree smashes your truck, you have a right to cut it up a bit."

I pulled my little tiny pocket knife out of my backpack and Dad laughed at me.

"Good to see you're prepared," he said.

"I also have water, a couple energy bars, an emergency blanket, the whistle you always made me carry, and a wind jacket."

"Great. Let's see if you can find a way into the wreckage of my truck and see what we have there."

I walked up to the bent and broken truck. The door looked okay, but all the jerking and cranking I did wouldn't open it. The window across the back was broken out but the tree was right up against the opening and the roof was partly smashed down there. Next I tried the driver's door. The roof on that side was caved in even more and the door was immovable. When I got back to the passenger side, Dad was there with a big rock.

"Do you want to do the honors?" he asked, holding out a rock and motioning toward the window.

"No way!" I said. I couldn't imagine smashing a rock through Dad's truck window.

"Are you sure? There won't be many chances for you to smash a window with my permission."

"Huh uh," I shook my head. This couldn't be real. Dad couldn't really want me to smash his window. I watched him roll closer to the truck and hoist the rock.

"Wait. If it really has to be done...I guess I could try."

Dad smiled and handed me the rock. He rolled back a bit. I threw the rock from about three feet away and it smashed into the window and fell to the ground. The window was shattered but it was still hanging in place. I lifted the rock again and heaved it through the window. This time it landed on the seat with a pile of shattered glass. I had to smile. That felt really good. Dad handed me a stick and I cleaned the remaining pieces of glass off the window frame. I pulled my headlamp out of my pack and put it on. Then I climbed in after the rock.

The inside of Dad's truck had looked like a hurricane hit it even before the tree fell on it. He constantly threw stuff behind the seats and rarely removed anything. I began to dig through the stash. The first thing I grabbed turned out to be the most important. I actually pulled out an old sleeping bag. I don't think it had been used as a sleeping bag for years. It was one of the old flannel ones. All of our newer ones are slick, shiny, lightweight, backpacking bags. This one felt way more comfortable. I remembered sitting on it as a blanket last Fourth of July. I shoved it out the window and continued to dig around. I found two old shirts that Dad had been using for rags. I was sure we would need all the clothing we could to keep warm tonight. I tossed those out the window also. There was a thin blanket that had paint all over it, and a pair of work gloves. Finally, I found a small pack by Dad's seat. He sometimes attached this to his wheelchair, and I knew it contained his catheters and supplies. I was about to climb back out when Dad told me to check the pocket in his door for a knife. There was a big, single blade, pocket knife there. I carried that with me as I slid back out the window.

"Geez Dad, that was like a goldmine."

"I can't believe your mom thinks I should clean out that truck. She thinks this stuff is junk can you believe it? See if you can cut a few branches with that knife and let's haul this stuff to camp."

I took Dad's knife and cut off about 12 small branches. Then I piled the shirts and blankets onto his lap and wrapped the sleeping bag over my shoulders. I had Dad wear my headlamp, and I gathered up an armload of branches and followed him down the fire road.

It wasn't far to Wienie Roast Rock, but it took us a while with our loads in the dark. Once there, I took the headlamp from Dad and scouted the layout. The branches were barely enough for one of us. I arranged them and then piled the blanket, my emergency blanket, and the sleeping bag to the side. I was starting to shiver a little bit and Dad noticed.

"Put on one of these old shirts. You don't want to get really cold and then have to try to warm up."

I slipped on a shirt, and pulled my windjacket out of my pack. The shirt was way too big and bunched up inside my windjacket, so it looked like I had a big puffy warm jacket on. Dad slipped on the other old shirt.

"I'll go back and get some more pine boughs," I said.

Dad looked around. There wasn't much that he could do until we had all the pine boughs.

"I guess I'll just sit here. With only one light it'll be easier for you to go back without me. Just be real careful with the knife."

"Okay." I started up the fire road holding the folded up knife in my hand. The beam from my LED headlamp barely lit two steps in front of me. It threw just enough light to make shadows to the sides. About 50 yards from Dad, I turned to look back. Obviously, I could only see two feet away from me. Dad was completely gone in the darkness. I turned back to the road and walked on. I started to get a little bit freaked. I kept turning my head to light up the woods beside me, but I really couldn't see past the first tree. I knew the darkness extended into the woods that went on for probably a hundred miles on one side and probably four miles back to town on the other. I felt so tiny. I started thinking about all the animals that would be in that much woods. Once a forest service guy came to our school to talk about mountain lions. He said that if we've hiked much in these woods, we have been trailed by a mountain lion. He said they like to walk parallel to you in the woods. They just kind of follow along beside you to check out who you are and what you are doing in their woods. Eventually they get bored and take off. Ever since his talk, when I'm in the woods alone, I hear things walking beside me. It was worse in the night because I knew it could be very close beside me.

I stopped and listened. I was getting more scared the more I thought about it. I opened the knife and started walking a little faster. Finally, I came to the clearing and the downed tree. I got right to work to take my mind off the dark woods. I chose a place near the top of the tree and just started hacking off branches. I had worked out a system with the first batch. Sort of whittling away at the branch first, allowed me to cut through it much faster. That technique, and the fact that I was scared and really wanted to get back with Dad, made the second batch go quickly. Then, I thought of him just sitting in the dark by himself in a wheelchair. I felt silly for being scared. I could move. I had a flashlight and a knife. He was stuck in a chair in the dark.

As soon as I had a full arm load, I headed back to Dad. This time I was able to focus on carrying the branches and getting back, and I didn't worry about the noises in the woods.

"Hey Dad," I yelled as I got close. He didn't answer until I was right up next to him. When my light hit his face, I could see that he was smiling.

When he finally answered, his voice was very soft. "Hey kid, what an awesome night. I was just sitting here listening to the darkness. It's amazing how many sounds you can hear. Something big flew right past my head. There's a lot of action off in that direction." He pointed to my right, and I stepped left. "I could even hear a couple of cars on the road to town. It's amazing to think of people sitting in those cars with the windows up and the radio blasting missing all that's going on out here."

"And driving home to their nice warm beds," I added.

Dad looked up. "We'll be fine. We didn't get to go backpacking at all last year. We're due for a night out."

"Okay." I dropped the load of branches beside the blankets. Then I got on my knees and spread the branches under the overhanging rock. Next, I spread the old, paint blanket on top of them. I laid out the sleeping bag and my emergency blanket at the foot of the paint blanket. I figured we would lie on the paint blanket and cover up with the bag and the emergency blanket. I stood back up and looked at Dad. "I guess I should go to the bathroom before we go to bed."

"Alright," he said. "Why don't you go and then give me the light and I'll go. I'll need the light to use the catheter."

"Okay." I grabbed some toilet paper out of my pack, laid my pack by the side of our makeshift bed, and stepped off into the woods; away from where Dad pointed out the "action".

When I came back, I gave Dad the flashlight. He pulled a catheter package out of the small bag on his wheelchair and placed it in his lap. Then he rolled up the road.

It was too dark to see anything without the light. I crawled around on the blanket trying to pack down the pine boughs a little.

"That was an adventure," Dad said as he rolled back into camp. He parked his wheelchair right up against the blanket and locked his brakes. Then he scooted himself forward, used his arms to pull his legs out in front of him, then lowered his butt down onto his footrests. He ended up in a really awkward position with his legs kind of scootched up under him. He teetered there for a moment, then smiled and just sort of dove and rolled onto the blanket. Together we moved his legs and scooted him onto one side of our bed. I helped secure the sleeping bag and blanket over him, and bunched up some of the pine branches under his head for a sort of pillow. Next I settled myself in beside him. It was really pretty cozy. The rock provided a half-roof and enough shelter on the sides to block most of the wind. We could hear the wind in the trees, but didn't feel much in our cozy little camp.

CHAPTER 17:
LISTENING TO DAD

I propped my head up on some branches and tried to think of what to say. I wanted to try to salvage this outing. I felt so bad about Dad's truck. I just couldn't find the right words. While I was still struggling, Dad spoke.

"I think it's pretty cool that you've been coming out here. And you're climbing really well. In the future, however, I do want you to tell us when you plan to ride out here. We really need to know whenever you're out climbing or out in the woods. You might even score a cell phone"

"Okay Dad. I'm so glad you came out with me. I'm so sorry about your truck." He laughed again. I said, "I can't believe you laughed when you saw it. You love that truck."

"I do love that truck. But it sure did look pathetic under that tree."

"Are you going to be able to get another one?"

"It was insured so it will be covered. I don't know if they'll pay for the window you broke though."

"Daaad."

"I'll be getting something, but it won't be another truck."

"Why not? Are you going to get a CAR?"

Dad laughed again. "Hard to imagine me with a car huh? But yes, I will get some kind of car. Climbing up into that truck is no easy task. I always thought it was worth it, but my physical therapist says that most paraplegics wreck their shoulders and end up with chronic shoulder pain. I was already thinking that I needed to trade in the truck. I'm gonna be relying on these shoulders to do a lot of work for the rest of my life."

"I wish you wouldn't talk like that."

"Like what?"

"Like you're giving in to your injury. You're letting it completely change who you are. You're giving up way too easy. No truck. No outdoor activities. Come on, don't you miss it? Don't you get a little crazy thinking about walking or riding a bike? I couldn't stand it if I couldn't walk. Do you think about it all day?"

"Maybe once in a while, when something is just out of reach, but not really. Walking is so far gone, so utterly impossible that I don't really long for it. I am, however, extremely thankful and happy that I did every single thing that I did on my legs while they worked. Every early morning bike ride when it was hard to get out of the warm bed and go out into the frosty morning, each time we grabbed snacks and water bottles and went for a hike. It would have been so much easier to hang around the house or watch TV. Now, I'm so grateful that we did all the things we did, and I have so many great memories.

"But why stop now. You're out here. Why haven't you come out for over a year? I know you can't ride your mountain bike or rock climb. But there are a lot of fire roads and trails that are wide and smooth enough for you. Heck, those are the only trails that Mom even likes. You could come out with her. You know you love the woods. You could kayak or canoe. They make a cross country skiing contraption. You could try that. You just watch TV and watch Walter practice football. Don't you want to do stuff anymore?" I was talking faster and louder as I went. I was practically frantic at the end, trying to talk him into getting out. I tried to keep talking because I knew I was about to start crying. I looked at Dad and he was just sitting there smiling. Instead of crying, I got angry. Chair flippin' angry.

"It's not funny," I yelled. "You don't even like TV that much and what's with football PRACTICE! You never used to go to any practices. You're turning into one of those middle age couch potatoes you said you would never be. I don't even see you anymore. It's bad enough that you can't walk, but now you don't even get out. I hate this. I hate it and it's not okay. I don't care what Walter says. We should not just try to entertain you and let you sit in the stands. You need to do stuff. I need you to do stuff." I hadn't looked at him again during my tirade. I was afraid I was hurting him, but it just all came busting out. When I did look, he wasn't smiling, but he had this caring look on his face that melted me from wanting to hit him to hugging him. I leaned my head against his chest and soaked his shirt with tears. He just stroked my hair and held me for a long time.

"I do need to get out" he said after a time. "I've been thinking of things I can do. I'm so glad we came out here today." We sat in silence for a while longer.

"Have you been angry for a while?" he asked.

"I guess so. Walter has been telling me not to be angry, but I didn't think I was. When he accused me of being angry, I got mad at him but otherwise I thought you all were acting weird and I was the only one dealing with it." I actually cracked a little smile. "I did get angry early on. I found Mom crying in the hospital hallway. She told me about the drunk that hit you and how he was in his room laughing about it.

"I got chair-flippin angry and stormed into his room."

"No way."

"Way," I said.

"What did you do?"

"Well, remember that time in the drive-thru when that car cut us off and you walked up to the driver's door?"

"You kicked his sideview mirror?"

"Well, I was just about as smooth. I stood in his room thinking about breaking a cane over his face. Then I remembered you and that rear-view mirror. Next thing I knew, I had been standing there daydreaming for a long time and I just turned and walked out."

"What a dork," Dad laughed.

"Yeah, well I came by it honestly." I elbowed him in the ribs.

We both lay there quietly for a while. Then Dad started talking about his legs.

"You know, I do think about my legs a lot. Sometimes I worry that they are lonely, feel abandoned. They spasm. Sometimes they spasm a lot. I can see that something is going on with them, but I can't tell what it is. It's like they need to tell me something, but I can't get the message. Just like I can't tell them to move."

I listened. I realized I hadn't listened or heard him talk about his injury ever.

"I've really been spending all my time in therapy. It's about time to cut back. When I finish a day of therapy, I'm so totally drained that I can't even think about another activity. I just go home and collapse; sometimes in front of the TV. It's the walking with the crutches that's the real killer."

So much for listening.

"You what? You walked with crutches?"

"Yeah, I've been working with those forearm crutches for the past few weeks. I can make it a few steps, all shaky and sweaty."

"Daddy, you can walk. You're going to walk. I knew it. I knew you wouldn't be stuck in that chair." I practically flung myself at him to give him a big hug. I think tears were streaming down my face. I know tears were streaming down my face when he peeled me off of him to say I was wrong.

"No," he said. "I'm not walking. I'm not going to walk."

"Don't say that Dad. You just said you were up on crutches. You don't give up. You don't quit. If anyone can beat this thing you can."

"I will beat this thing," he answered. "But, I'm going to beat it in a chair. I'm not going to spend my life in physical therapy trying to do the impossible."

"But Dad, you can do it. You're already walking some steps. You just need to get a little stronger." I couldn't believe he was saying he was going to give up. How could someone give up on walking?

"I can only walk a few steps with full braces on both legs. I need two people to help me up, and one to walk with me and one to move my chair behind me. My hands and arms are fully engaged with the crutches and get exhausted in just a few steps. I need my arms to function. I can't waste them on a hopeless cause. I can zip across the room in my chair with no help. I can carry stuff with me. When I stop therapy, I'll have time with you and Walter and Mom. I can get out here more. I can start living my life again."

Tears streaming down my face was an understatement at this point. I was sobbing.

"Dad, I'm so sorry. I've been so mad at you for not doing stuff. I didn't realize how much you were working in therapy. Walter said I was angry, and I couldn't see it. But I was wrong. It just seemed like you had given up on life. On all the things you've always loved to do. TV and watching Walter seemed like your only interests. I'm sorry. You were working so hard, and I thought you had just given up. Don't quit therapy. Maybe your walking will get better. We can start doing other stuff next year or the year after that. Whatever it takes. You could walk."

"I won't walk babe. My doctors and therapists have said it all along. The crutches were just for exercise.... and to prove to me that I had tried everything. Now I know I have. I can move on and not feel like I gave in too easily. I really want my life back. Come on. This is great. I've missed being out here so much. I never was much for working out in a gym. Look what I've been missing. You're becoming a climber. I can't miss out on that." After a brief silence, he finished, "My legs carried me for 36 years, I can carry them for a while."

I lay there for quite a while thinking about what he said. Crying for a while, then, sucking it up only to break down and cry again. Finally, I seemed to run out of tears. I stared out into the woods.

"Dad, look at that. It's getting light out. It's only like nine o'clock."

"Yeah, the moon's coming up. It was a full moon a couple of nights ago."

"How do you know?"

"On a full moon, the moon comes up right at sunset. Every day it rises about 40 minutes later. In a little bit it will be quite bright out here."

I snuggled down beside him and tucked the old sleeping bag in beside me. He put his arm around me and squeezed my shoulder. There was so much power in that touch. Not just the strength in his hand, but I could feel an energy coming through him. He had always been like that, but it was stronger now. I remember when I was little and would get scared at night. He and Mom would never give me permission to sleep in their bed, but once in a while I'd talk them in to letting me sleep beside the bed on the floor. Dad would usually send me back to my room so I would try to sneak in. I'd tiptoe down the hallway dragging my quilt and holding my pillow. If I could get set up on the floor without Dad noticing, I could spend the night there. Sometimes, after I was all settled in, he would lower his hand and I would hold it or snuggle my face against it. It always took away the fear. It felt so secure and comforting. I liked to think that I could feel his soul or spirit. It was some kind of energy coming through his body. Now, on the ground in the woods, I felt it again. Stronger now. It was like his soul that had been spread throughout his whole body was now concentrated in the top half of his body that still worked. So much spirit, so much energy in half a body felt really strong, and really good.

"Dad?"

"Yeah babe?"

"You could play linebacker for the Oklahoma Sooners."

"Thanks babe. I think that's one dream that I'm finally letting go."

With the wind still howling through the trees, I went to sleep easily.

CHAPTER 18:
NIGHT STORIES

I must have woken up about an hour later. The moon was bright overhead. Dad appeared to be asleep. I breathed in the musty, pine smell of the ground by my face, and listened to the night. Dad's breathing was rhythmic and slow. Far off in the trees the wind was blowing hard. I listened to it getting closer, then heard the needles drop and felt the breeze. What sounded like a freight train far off whimpered out to a little whisp in our sheltered spot. Pine needles and cones occasionally dropped as the wind moved over us. There were almost no animal sounds at this time of night, but I reacted to each movement of a branch as if it was an approaching bear. Really, I wasn't too scared. I used to have a lot of trouble on backpacking trips because I would be so afraid. I especially had trouble the first night of a camping trip in the woods. I would lie awake for hours listening for something or someone to approach our camp. I guess it's sad that I was most worried about people, even when we were miles out in the wilderness. I liked campsites off the trail where no one was likely to stumble across us or to see us from a distance. I know it's not rational, but I always felt more comfortable after sleeping in a place once. It's like I think that if a place is safe one night it will always be safe. Whenever we return to a camping spot, I sleep great. So, I always try to get us back to familiar places. Dad always wants to explore some place new of course. The most reassuring thing in the woods is my dad. He seems to know what to do, and I always feel sure that things will be alright because they always are with him. Once he even said it. He said, "things seem to work out for me." And I try to keep that in mind when I get a little afraid and he's with me. Funny, I still think it's true, even after his injury. He got run over by a drunk. He's paralyzed. He can't pee or poop normally and yet, everyone who knows him probably still feels like "things work out for him." How does he do that?

I looked out into the woods around camp. Even though I'd never camped at the Ravine, I'd been there so often that I felt pretty safe. Still, I must have woken up a half dozen times thinking I was hearing something, usually footsteps. I would prop my head up and stare into the darkness. Every tree seemed to have someone partially hidden behind it. Eventually, I would tire of staring at nothing and convince myself to lie down and close my eyes. Then I would just listen for a while until I could convince myself that I was hearing a branch move or that the footsteps were moving away, and I would fall back asleep.

One of those times, just as I was about to go back to sleep, I noticed that Dad was awake and watching me.

"Dad, remember the night we backpacked to Howl Lake?"

"The footsteps in the water?"

"Yeah, I'll never forget lying under that tarp, listening to those giant steps coming towards us – sploosh, sploosh, sploosh. I think it was the darkest night we ever slept out."

"So you couldn't have seen what it was even if you did poke your head out of your bag?"

"I wasn't about to move," I said. "I was trying not to breathe."

"You wouldn't even let me shine a flashlight at it."

"I didn't want it to know we were there. What do you think it was?"

"I'm sure it was a deer....or a bear."

I looked over to see him smiling at me. "I'm pretty sure you didn't mention a bear when we were out there."

"You were frightened enough."

"I think it was Bigfoot. Anyway, that's what I say when I tell this story to my friends at sleepovers. I make it really scary. They always love it." Dad smiled and I continued, "But my best sleepover story is Walter in Mom's pink pants."

"What?" asked Dad.

"Remember? All four of us backpacked to Mule Creek Meadow. We were just going for one night and nobody brought extra clothes but Mom. Walter spilled that potato, broccoli, soup stuff all over his pants. He left them hanging over a stump all night and in the morning they were all slimy and crawling with ants. Mom had the only extra pair of pants, some pink stretchy things, and you convinced Walter to wear them saying that no one would see him way out in the wilderness. But, on the hike out, we passed like 40 people who all laughed at Walter. My friends love that story."

"That's a good story, but I'm not sure it's very accurate."

"What do you mean?" I tried to sound innocent.

"I'm pretty sure your mom has never owned a pair of pink, stretchy, pants, and we've never seen more than 4 or 5 people on a hike out of the woods."

I thought about this for a bit. "You know my language arts teacher, Mrs. Saraceno, told us about this thing called a 'poetic license.'"

"And you think that's a license to put pink pants on your brother in front of 40 witnesses and to turn a deer into Bigfoot?"

"Yes, I think that's it." I smiled and Dad chuckled. We were both quiet for a little bit.

Eventually, Dad spoke. "I think my favorite story is your first climb. Do you remember it?"

"Mostly, I think I just remember you telling it. Tell me again."

"We went to Brighton Bluff with Danny. I think you were about six. The rock was at the top of a tall ridge. You hiked all the way up by yourself. The slope at the base of the climbs was really steep. It dropped off a couple of hundred feet and I couldn't find a safe place for you to sit while Danny and I climbed. You had this little, full-body harness and we harnessed you up and tied you to a tree with about six feet of rope. You plopped down on the ground with a Barbie doll and a couple of coloring books and did great, until your Barbie slipped down out of your reach. When I finished my climb, you were six feet below your tree, hanging upside down trying to rescue your Barbie."

"I remember that part. I was afraid she was gone for ever."

"Well, Danny climbed down and rescued her while I untied from the rope. It was a good warm up for his next task, which was to rescue you from your climb. We put you on a 5.6 thinking you would work the first couple of moves off the ground. But, once you got started, you scampered right on up. You must have been thirty feet up when you climbed on to a small ledge to rest. The longer you sat on the ledge, the farther back you scooted. Pretty soon all we could see were the soles of your little climbing shoes sticking out to the edge of the ledge. Then, you announced that you weren't coming down. You didn't cry or panic or get upset. You just calmly explained that you were not going near the edge, and you liked it just fine where you sat.

"We tried everything; bargaining, begging, yelling. We even tried to get you to climb higher hoping that you would let us lower you from somewhere else. I'll bet you sat there for half an hour. Finally, Danny free soloed up to your ledge. I was really worried that you might kick him off when he got there."

"Dad..."

"Well, you were scared. But you didn't. He climbed up beside you and clipped into your harness. Then, he picked you up, and I lowered you together. You put such a head lock on him I was afraid he'd pass out before I could get you to the ground. For about a year after that, Danny was your big hero.

"After that, I never put you on climbs with ledges. And now look at you. You're climbing overhangs."

We both sat quietly for a while remembering old climbing stories.

"Dad?"

"Yeah."

"We haven't made any new stories for almost two years now."

"You know, I think we're working on a pretty good one right here."

"Yeah," I smiled. "And let's not stop with this one."

"Definitely," he answered. "Now get some sleep kid."

I kissed his cheek and rolled over on my side. I went right to sleep, but still woke up several more times during the night.

CHAPTER 19: OUT
OF THE WOODS

T owards morning, the birds began to sing. Actually, it sounded more like they were arguing. Even with all their racket, I easily fell back to sleep. I thought they would get quiet or leave if anything dangerous was around. I probably got my best sleep in the last two hours before morning. When I did wake up it was fully light. Dad was lying on his stomach looking out into the woods.

"Hey sleepy head," he said without looking over at me. "You missed a great sunrise."

"I thought you'd have breakfast ready," I countered.

He smiled and pointed at two energy bars lying on a rock a couple of feet from our heads. It took me a couple of minutes to realize that he couldn't have gotten up and put them there. In fact, I knew we didn't have any more bars. I looked to Dad for an explanation. He just shrugged his shoulders.

"Oh my gosh! He was here." I sat up and looked around. I was really freaked out. Then I relaxed, and then I even laughed. Dad was just watching me, waiting for an explanation.

"Strider," I started. "He lives in the woods a couple of ridges towards town. He must have come by during the night."

"And he gave us some energy bars?" Dad asked with amusement.

"Yeah." I went on to tell him about my first scary, accidental trip into his camp and my energy bar tradition.

"You've been quite the adventurer," was Dad's response. "Shall we have some breakfast?"

I crawled out and grabbed the bars. We ate still huddled in our shelter. The sun was hitting us by the time we finished, and there was no wind. We started to warm up nicely. I really had to pee and realized that Dad would too.

"Can I run to the bathroom and then help you up?"

"Sure."

I scurried off into the woods, away from the direction of Strider's camp.

When I came back, we had the project of getting Dad back into his chair. Dad pointed out a rock the size of a small footstool a few feet away from our camp. I parked the chair up against it, and Dad scooted backwards on his butt over to the rock. With his back against the rock, he put his hands on the rock behind him and lifted himself onto the rock. Then he reached backwards to the chair. I tried to hold the chair steady while he tried to lift himself up into it. The problem was that now he had to drag his legs over the rock, and that was not easy. His pants got snagged on the rock a couple of times, and then one leg fell off to the side of the rock and just about tipped us all over. Dad kept working at it, and I kept wrestling the chair. Eventually he was all the way back into the chair. It took him a second to catch his breath, then he arranged his legs on his footpeg and high fived me.

"Not exactly smooth, but I'm in the chair," he said with some satisfaction. I handed him his catheter supplies, and then I began to roll up the sleeping bag and blanket while he moved away to "empty his bladder" as the nurses always called it in rehab. When I thought he might be done, I loaded up the blankets and started up the fire road. I saw him ahead of me struggling to get his pants back up. It looked really hard to pull up your pants while you were sitting in a chair on wheels. I waited from a little ways away until he was finished.

"Well, should we try to walk out or wait by the truck until someone shows up?" I asked.

"I don't know," he said. "Let's get to the truck and play it by ear."

The truck still looked pathetic crunched under the tree. I realized as I looked at the tree that it blocked the entire road and clearing. I could walk around it into the woods, but there was no easy way for Dad to get past the tree in his chair. We went to the side of the clearing closest to the truck. When the tree fell over, the roots from the other side were ripped out and now they stuck eight or ten feet into the air. Behind them was a small crater. I left Dad by the truck and walked into the woods. It looked to me like we would have to clear a path for him around the hole left by the roots. It seemed to be our only option. On the other side of the clearing the tree extended way into the woods with broken branches jutting out in all directions.

"I'll start clearing a path," I told Dad. He just nodded and rolled back to look at his truck.

I had cleared about 6 feet into the woods when I heard a very noisy truck coming up the fire road. I hurried back to Dad, and we watched together in amazement as a tow truck pulled up on the other side of the tree. Jack Johnson, an old climber friend of Dad's hopped out of the truck. He had been over to our house a few times. Dad always talked about how Jack never changed. I gradually understood that that wasn't necessarily a good thing. He seemed to have a different job every time he showed up. He spent summers climbing and winters skiing and, if he kept a job for more than six months, he would save up enough money for a mountaineering trip and would quit the job to take the trip. He always seemed to be in a good mood and always had fun stories. Often, Dad wished that Jack didn't share the stories when Walter and I were around.

He let out a long whistle as he climbed over the tree and surveyed Dad's truck. "Don't worry dude, we can fix it. I've got some tools." Then he busted out laughing. He walked around the truck assessing the damage. He seemed to spend an especially long time looking at the window I had broken. Then he stepped back, kicked the door and declared, "This fucking fucker is fucked."

"What are you doing out here?" Dad asked, ignoring Jack's assessment of his truck.

"That homeless guy that collects cans came by this morning and said someone needed a tow truck out here. But you don't need a tow truck. You need a chain saw and a big recycle bin for that hunk of aluminum."

"And a ride back to town," Dad added.

"That I can do Jeff. Dude, are you alright? Did you really spend the night out here?"

"Yeah, it wasn't too bad. You and I have bivouacked in much worse condition than this." He gestured at his legs.

"Too true man, too true."

"Besides," said Dad. "I had a much more competent partner here than when it was you and me."

Jack looked over at me and smiled. "Once again you make a good point. You know I was out here the other day and saw her send *Squeeze Play*. Like father like daughter. Except, she made it look easy. I remember when you put that problem up. Your big old butt dragged the ground all the way across that problem. Didn't you have to dig out a path so that you could clear the ground at the crux?"

Dad glanced at me looking mighty guilty.

"Wait a minute," I said. "You put up *Squeeze Play*? Wait a minute! You NAMED *Squeeze Play*?"

"Let's get this path done and get out of here," tried Dad.

"What were you thinking? Baseball? What a sucky name."

Jack joined in. "She's got you there bro. Considering the way you dragged your ass on it, I always thought you should call it..."

"Never mind," Dad interjected. "It's too late now. I'm sure there were better names."

"I'm sure there weren't any worse," I said, which made Dad and Jack share a laugh.

With Jack's help it didn't take long to clear a path and help

Dad get his chair to the other side of the tree. I climbed into the middle of tow truck and stuffed the blankets behind the seat. Here was a truck with even more junk piled into it than Dad's. Dad gave Jack some very specific instructions for helping him into the truck, and then Jack fastened the wheelchair onto the back of the tow truck. Soon we were bouncing up the road headed to town.

Jack and Dad talked about their climbing days and Jack said he always figured he would have been the one to end up in a wheelchair. Dad agreed and they shared another laugh. Jack offered to go back out for the truck with some friends and a chainsaw after work. He said he would look for a junk dealer that would take the truck. I listened for a while thinking they sounded a lot like Kyle and Michael. Then I kind of drifted off. Man was I tired. I didn't really sleep, but don't remember much of the drive until we were turning on to our street. We piled out of the truck and watched Jack drive away. Suddenly I got a picture of the two of us in the driveway with our baggy old shirts and light coat of dust. Dad must have had the same image.

"We better get in and get cleaned up before your mom and brother come home. We could scare them half to death looking like this."

"Yeah, and then let's get some breakfast."

"Definitely."

By the time we had both showered and met back in the kitchen it was lunch time.

"I liked the breakfast idea, but now I'm thinking pizza," said Dad.

"Pizza takes a long time to make."

Dad picked up the phone. "Get real. What do you want on it."

Half an hour later we were sitting at the table snarfing pizza when Mom and Walter got home. We listened politely while they told us about the game and their little adventures in Collinwood. Finally, Mom asked about the truck. Dad launched into the whole story making it sound like it was his idea to go out to the Ravine. He laughed again when he described the squished wreckage of his truck. We were both laughing hysterically when he tried to tell them about *Squeeze Play/Lowdown* and clearly, Mom and Walter saw nothing funny and thought we were both nuts.

We only let them have the last two pieces of pizza when they agreed to order another one. It seemed like we spent most of the afternoon around the table eating and telling stories. We hadn't...actually, I, hadn't been acting like that much of a family for a long time. It was a really nice afternoon.

CHAPTER 20: A NEW NORMAL

Things changed after that. Not suddenly. In fact, I can't say I noticed the change while it happened. Looking back though, I can follow the progression. Winter came and buried the mountains in snow. Walter finished the football season. I became more aware of how much time Dad spent in therapies. And, I noticed as he gradually decreased that time. It was hard to see him give it up, but he really did increase other activities when he let up on therapy. A lot of those activities were exactly the things I had been hoping for. What an idiot I was to think he would turn into a couch potato. I really felt bad that he was giving up therapy and hoped I hadn't pressured him.

Dad got a cross-country ski device and we did a couple of family outings. It was a little like a seat on skis that he propelled with poles and steered by leaning his upper body. He did great on the flats, risked his life on the downhills, and Walter and I pushed and pulled him up a couple of steep inclines.

In early spring Dad started working part-time at the bike shop. They were transitioning from the ski season back to bikes, and he got to assemble some of the new bikes and help with setting up for the spring tune-ups. He seemed to love the place. Sometimes I rode over to the shop after school. I liked hanging out there too. A lot of the bikers were also climbers, so I worked to build my climbing contacts. Dad helped. He hooked me up with a women's climbing group. About once a month, I got out to the park with them. Climbing with the girls was great. They were really supportive, and fun, and some of them were small enough for me to belay. I think Dad was more comfortable having me climb with that group than with the Ravine guys. I still think I'll get out there with the boys soon.

Dad's bike shop sponsored a big mountain bike race in the spring. He helped run the race by working at the registration booth. He talked me into entering and I got third place. Okay, so there were only eight girls in my division. Still, it was way cool to cross the finish line with my dad there cheering me on. I'm not supposed to know, but I'm pretty sure I'm getting my first "new" mountain bike for my birthday. I think Dad gets a pretty good discount at the shop. I hope he gets his hand-bike first.

Mom was able to quit the part-time job she didn't like and increase hours at the job she did like. Lots of small changes but they really added up.

Towards the end of the school year it all kind of came together. I was setting the table and Mom was cooking. Walter was supposedly doing homework on the couch with the TV and the radio on. Dad was due home from work (the bike shop) any minute. I rounded the table placing forks and knives when I suddenly felt like I could see the room from outside. What I saw caught me by surprise. We had returned to normal. Not the normal we were before Dad's injury. Obviously, things would never go back like they had been. However, we had established a new normal. Most nights we were all home for supper. We knew what the others were up to and when to expect them. There was enough of a consistent routine that we knew when one of us was going through something extra. We had a new normal; and it was nice. Oh yeah, another nice thing; I started dating Kyle. Well, not dating exactly since Mom and Dad won't let me date yet. But, I meet him at school dances and we've been hanging out together at basketball games. Once he told me that I seem really independent and brave. He said he likes that.

"Is there something wrong with the forks honey?"

Once again, I had spaced out, this time holding the forks out over the table. Normal enough for me.

"Mom? Do I seem independent and brave?"

Mom laughed. She laughed at me.

"Mom?" I asked.

"Honey, you are the most independent kid I know. We've been through a lot in the last couple years, and you have pretty much insisted on handling it alone."

"But I didn't do it alone Mom. You took care of us all. And I was miserable until I talked with Dad, and even talking with Walter helped." I looked over to the living room to make sure Walter didn't hear me. He was oblivious."

"Talking with Dad and your brother was the brave part," she said.

"Really, I think I tried to avoid it."

"Those conversations are never easy. But they were helpful, huh?"

Just then we heard the front door open and close. Dad rolled into the kitchen.

"Gather 'round family. I have news," he proclaimed in a goofy announcer voice. Nobody "gathered 'round" but we all stopped and looked over at him.

He continued in his normal tone, "Mr. Pritchard has decided to move to Salem to develop a new store there. As of next month, I will be taking over all the management operations of the bike shop." Back to goofy announcer voice, "And it will be good for I am......." and placing his hands on his hips, he puffed up his chest and declared "I am, MIDDLE MANAGEMENT MAN!"

His pronouncement ended with a brief pause.

"Dad, you are such a Dork" I finally said.

"Yup, and don't you just love it," he smiled.

"Yes I do."

I really do.

That's my dad.

ACKNOWLEDGEMENT

Thanks to Bill Trueblood for all the support, encouragement, and suggestions as we worked at writing our books. Thanks to Shawndi Stahl for the thorough read-through, the help with the climbing sequences, and the climbing adventures we shared. The women in our little writing group at B&N helped me capture the voice of a 12-year-old girl and I appreciate that. Thanks again to my family for always being there for me. Thanks to Susan Fox Rogers for the quote. She is editor of "Solo: On Her Own Adventure," and author of the recently released, "Learning the Birds."